Copyright © Claude Dancourt 2014
http://www.claudedancourt.webs.com

ISBN (ebook): 978-0-9880313-7-1
ISBN (hard copy): 978-0-9880313-6-4

Cover Artist: Claude Dancourt
Editor: Lorelei Logsdon

Acknowledgments

I am very thankful to Ethan, Arya and Gabriele for their support and friendship. Also, Garry Rodgers offered great insights about guns and police habits. I hope he will forgive the liberty I took with some details. I'd also like to thank Lorelei for her careful editing. All mistakes that remain are my own.

The Isabella Gardner Heist occurred on the night of March 18, 1990. Two thieves entered the Museum pausing as Boston police officers. They stole thirteen works of art.

In April 2013, the FBI confirmed that they believe a crime organization from New England was involved. They also think that the stolen artwork was transported to Connecticut and/or Pennsylvania for sale. Up to this day, the artwork has not been found.

Claude Dancourt

RECKLESS ILLUSIONS

By

Claude Dancourt

Chapter 1

"If some people didn't call in favors and overload our lab, maybe we would be able to get some real work done."

"I'm not 'calling in favors,' Ian! I'm paying for the use of forensics, just like the police do! And I assure you—"

"You're buying your way in, you mean."

Neve gawped, at a loss for words. He nearly implied, no he *did* imply that she bribed the technicians at the lab, and that her work was not important, and now… Why was he so unfair? She did the same job that he did. Just because she didn't wear a badge… Old images yoked the anger boiling up in her veins. What happened was not her fault. She tried to do some good around her. Her eyes watered, the tears burning and unwelcomed. She was going to kill him. She was going to bloody kill him as soon as Stefan released her arm so she could get up.

Ian used the delay to turn away with a shrug. He strolled to a safe distance, while she fought to get rid of Stefan's grasp. Neve hissed, "I'm calm, Stefan, let me go."

The lie earned her a knowing look.

"Sure you are. But I like holding you close."

The boyish grin wiped away some of her turmoil. She inhaled heavily and nodded. Stefan freed her wrist then considered the slender woman on the other side of the corner booth.

"Why don't you tell him why you left the Academy?"

Neve bobbed her shoulders. The gesture was quite similar to the one her nemesis had given her a minute ago before he fled the battlefield.

"I didn't graduate, so what? I don't care about what His Majesty thinks. You don't need a badge to be a good investigator."

She straightened up on her seat. Stefan tried again.

"You're constantly arguing about the 'PI/cop' thing. If Ian knew why you quit, maybe he'd stop…"

"We're not arguing. You can't argue with someone who thinks he's always right. Plus, I won't give him the pleasure of an explanation. He's just abusive. I'm sure he's going to bully some poor tech to have his stuff analyzed first anyway."

Stefan sighed. They came to the Bottom Stone Pub for lunch every time they needed to drop a request or collect results from the only forensic lab in town. But it seemed that each time, Ian Braich was there. And each time, he and Neve found a way to restart the battle that opposed them for years.

Their cases had them cross each other's paths now and then. Every encounter resulted in blinding fireworks. The son of the legendary Ian Braich Sr couldn't get over the fact that Neve ran a successful private investigation agency. Given that Neve was female and incredibly attractive probably didn't help. As for Neve, Ian's abrupt manners and haughty tone wore on her nerves so that she never failed to answer the provocation. At least this time Stefan had caught her in time before she did something

2

she would regret -- like that right hook that had landed into Stefan's shoulder once. He'd had a bruise for days afterward, and Neve had winced every time he grimaced.

Ian would never let the chance to charge her with assault pass by. Stefan mumbled under his breath.

"I wonder what got his panties into a twist today…"

Neve snapped her fingers in front of his eyes. Stefan jolted.

"Sorry. I was thinking out loud."

"Yeah, I saw that. Enough with Braich. I want to appreciate lunch. Do you want some?"

"Hum?"

"The fries, Stefan. If I eat all those, I'm going to be sleepy all afternoon. Be a sweetheart and help me."

Stefan shook his head, pushing away thoughts about the temperamental detective to pop two French fries into his mouth.

Neve was like that. She stayed cool and professional when she worked. She fought tooth and nail when she felt threatened. And the rest of the time, she was uncomplicated and welcoming. He would always remember she had offered him a roof over his head and a job when he needed them the most. Stefan washed the last bite of his sandwich with a gulp of soda and asked, "So, what do we do next?"

"We have to check in for our results. I'd also like to talk to Mrs. Goblin once more. The police report was rather laconic, and apparently she wasn't very cooperative with the insurance inspector. Maybe she'll be in a better mood this time…"

Stefan grimaced. Neve pointed a warning finger toward his nose.

"I don't want to hear anything!"

"Oh come on… She really looks like a goblin… For someone whose first name ends with bella, that's terrible.

Have you seen her nose? Her teeth are sharper than a piranha's and she had a mole on her–"

Neve made a face.

"Ew... Thanks! Now I won't be able to look at her in the eyes when I talk to her."

"Well, her eyes are–"

"Stefan!" Neve bellowed.

Half the pub turned toward their corner, the other half fascinated by the weekend football results. Unfortunately, Ian Braich fell into the first category. His intense gaze mocked her from afar. Neve's gaze shot daggers at him, her cheeks flaming for the general attention, before she glared at her best friend/assistant.

"I could have done without more of his contempt, Stef'..."

He pouted, fluttering his lashes in his best sick-puppy expression. Neve smiled in spite of herself. The young man had a knack to whirl every situation into a laugh, even, and especially, when that moron Ian Braich was around.

She tried to remember the one time she had seen his father. Ian Braich Sr used to be the best cop in town, a man larger than life, with piercing gray eyes and a persuasive voice. So persuasive her older brother hadn't resisted, and climbed into the car waiting for them in front of the house...

The son didn't live up to the man's image. She felt sorry for his mother, and whoever shared his life -- if by chance he had managed to lure some unlucky woman into his bitter web for more than one night. Broad shoulders and stormy gray eyes didn't make up for ill-behavior, not at all. If only he would apologize for being rude once in a while, maybe she would step down, but he took a sick pleasure in worsening his case every time they met. His one-track mind placed private investigators only one step above bounty hunters, merely good enough to find lost pets or track cheating spouses. As for his opinion of working women...

Neve finished her coffee in one gulp. Ian Braich was abusive, contemptuous, and petty. He didn't deserve the time she spent raging after him. Next time, she would send Stefan by himself to the lab, and avoid the idiot altogether.

She retrieved her scarf and wrapped it around her neck before she proceeded to the cashier to take care of their bill. Fishing her wallet out of her purse, she cast a glance toward her friend. Stefan was battling with his sleeves. As far as she could tell, the jacket was winning. SendStefan by himself to the station and Lauren would look like the cat that got the cream. be like pouring milk in a cat's face. He would never survive the encounter.

She sighed. Hopefully the results the brilliant forensic leader had for her would compensate for enduring Ian's out of place wrath. One could only hope.

*

She had made of a fool of him in front of the whole pub! And then she had turned misty eyes on him so he felt like the worst man on earth for defending his case.

His phone rang, distracting Ian from his disturbing thoughts. He dismissed the infuriating beauty from his mind and took the call he'd been waiting for all morning.

"So?"

'Good afternoon to you to, Ian. I'm great, that's so nice of you to ask...'

"Not now, Lauren. Do you have my results?"

'Yes, I do.'

He gritted his teeth. The cute technician who ran the police lab loved torturing him nearly as much as she liked her gadgets. Entering her office was like stepping into James Bond's playroom. But after the confrontation with

Neve, he wasn't in the mood for any Casino Royale bluff. He barked, "Well, you are welcome to share."

A pregnant silence answered him, and for a heartbeat, he feared she'd hung up. Then he heard a ruffle of papers, as if she was looking through her documents, unsure what information to give him first. She knew perfectly well he desperately needed an ID on the body stuffed in the fourth tray at the morgue. The sooner he got a name, the better his chances to find a decent lead in this damned case.

The guy had been found in the Gallery Park a week ago, without his coat or his shoes. Of course, his wallet was also missing, which was not really a surprise. They found all too many like him since the recession had hit the country. People came to the city in hopes of a job, and ended up in the streets, out of resources and forgotten. Winter in these parts was merciless. A sad, but classic tragedy, until they had found a bullet hole when taking the corpse away. Then, it had become a homicide, and his current headache.

Lauren was still delaying and Ian felt his patience growing thin. He snapped, "I'm not getting any younger, Lauren."

'Or more amiable, as far as I can tell.'

Ian shoved his glove in his pocket with his free hand. The wind was biting into the fingers holding the phone. If it started snowing, his day would be complete. He forced his jaw to work.

"Please?"

'The database search came up empty. His fingerprints are not on file.'

He didn't bother asking for dental records identification. Without any idea who the body might be, this could take forever.

"Drugs?"

"Besides faint traces of Delta-9-THC metabolites and ethanol, nope, his blood was clean."

Ian felt an itch along his spine, which had nothing to do with the cold. He growled under his breath.

"Lauren…"

"Marijuana, Ian. The guy smoked weed, and he had a drink or two not long before dying. A strong alcohol, I would say, the ratio methyl-ethyl was–"

He interrupted her before she got lost again in her technical babbling.

"Thanks for the translation. What about the tattoo?"

'A Chinese symbol for luck. Top ten of the current requests in ink & pierce shops.'

"Damn it!"

The young man kicked the pole next to the stairs before him. The sharp pain in his toe made him curse again. Lauren sneered, "What was that?"

He could hear her laugh up her sleeve. Her lack of concern didn't improve his mood.

"Did you call me to tell me you failed or?"

'Ian, you requested to be advised as soon as I got the results.'

He had. But at the time he hoped the forensic would come up with something useful. Lauren was still haranguing him. Apparently, she was in league with Neve Lass for biting his head off today.

'Anyhow, that's up to you to go through the complete MP file. My report will be available tomorrow.'

This time she hung up without giving him enough time to put a word in edgewise. Lauren wasn't one to nurse a grudge, contrary to the stunning PI, so he didn't worry much about her ire. She hated coming up empty handed, and once in a while she decided he needed to be flogged for his no-nonsense kind of abrupt ways. She would come around in a day or two. That was about how long it was going to take him to go through the Missing persons list. Ian muttered under his breath, climbing the two steps that led inside the station. How much worse could it get, anyway? Feminist amateurism spoiled his lunch; he had a murder to solve without any clue on the victim…

"Braich! My office, now!"

Yeah, third time was the charm all right.

Chapter 2

Neve followed her unwilling hostess toward the living room.

The woman hadn't stopped frowning since she opened the door. Neve almost counted the fact she allowed her in as a victory. Insurance investigators were never popular, but that one was pushing the disliking to new heights.

"Mrs. Goblin, I only have a few questions, I promise I won't take too much of your time…"

A grunt answered her attempt.

"Tea?"

Neve cast a look toward the porcelain on display. The liquid was a muddy brown from the milk she had poured in it.

"No, thank you. "

"I already told you everything I know the last time. The company doesn't want to pay for my loss in full and they used every excuse to delay. I don't see the point in disturbing me."

The young woman swallowed the hidden insult, and looked around. Haydn's Flute Concerto in D poured from a radio or a television set, hidden in the heavily polished furniture. The embroidered cushions were impeccably set on the ottoman. Even the loveseats were neat. Neve looked for traces of an open book or half-finished crossword to no avail. Apart from the cup on a tray, the room was ready for a photography session for an Elle Décor Magazine special on Eighteenth-Century style. Even the paintings on the walls matched.

The older woman coughed not so discreetly. Her lips were pursed into a thin, hostile line. Neve forced herself to smile.

"I won't be long, I promise. I wanted to give you an update on our investigation and–"

The old bat scoffed.

"I don't need an update. What I want is my balance check."

Neve nodded. Her mouth hurt from the effort of keeping an obliging face. Stefan had just earned himself a week of chores for this.

"I understand, Mrs. Goblin. I'm certain the insurance company will honor their contract. It's just that the sum is important, so they want to understand exactly what happened."

"Be done with it, then. I have things to do. I can't spend the whole day in idle chitchat."

"Of course."

The woman picked up her cup with two fingers. She took a sip, and placed the delicate china back on the small plate. Neve flipped through the apps on her smartphone to find the recorder. The suspicious glare intensified.

"The police took notes."

"I'm not the police."

She hoped her retort would not antagonize the harpy further.

"Can you please tell me what you know about the collection, with your own words?"

*

Stefan hopped up the steps leading inside the building. He had whined and pleaded until Neve agreed to split their errands for the afternoon. So while Neve returned to interview the harpy in her nest, he simply was to collect the preliminary report they needed to finally move forward with their case.

The insurance company had agreed to pay the extra fees of a rushed analysis without a word. They were too anxious to know if they had to hand over a check of several hundred thousand dollars. *If* was the key word. X-ray, spectrometer, chemicals, scans, they had ordered the whole menu. Some analysis Lauren had admitted not having performed in years. Stefan nodded to himself. He knew the vivacious tech's tendency to paint a gloomy portrait of everything, so that her results would look miraculous afterward. He didn't really mind. His stomach always did a funny flip when she beamed in triumph.

The inside of the building was overheated. Stefan unhooked the first buttons of his parka while looking around. The first floor was buzzing. As usual, Bourque was yelling at someone. Stefan skirted to the stairs that led to the first floor before the Bull, as the crew called him, decided to trample on his next victim, namely himself. The man appreciated the external jobs the lab took even less than Ian.

The young man climbed up while pulling on his scarf.

"Wow, careful with that!"

He jumped, skidding on the polished steps. A large hand grabbed his collar to pull him up before he lost his footing completely. Stefan sighed in relief, craning his head back.

"Hi, Caleb!"

The technician released his jacket to secure a stack of files under one arm. Everyone else would have staggered under the load. Caleb's massive frame would make a cupboard look frail.

"Hey. You're here for the residues, I guess."

Stefan grinned at the underlying question.

"Yeap. Neve sent me to collect whatever you have."

He regretted mentioning his boss as soon as Caleb glowered, his lips pinched into a thin line, swallowed within his neatly trimmed beard. So, Neve had refused the dinner invitation... Suddenly, winning the argument of the task-splitting felt a little less like one. Stefan battled with his scarf once more. He repeated, "Yeah. I'm here for the results. If you have some. Do you?"

The man balanced the files under one forearm to punch the door open with his fist. Stefan hurried in after him, his mouth moving continuously to drown his misstep.

"So? What did you find? Tell me the hours we spent screening cinders and picking up scraps paid off. My back is still sore and I didn't even mention my kne–"

"Hi, Stefan. Tearing my assistant's ears off already?"

His cheeks flushed the bright shade of tomatoes.

"Oh, huh, Lauren, hello. How... Sorry."

He extracted one icy hand from his glove.

"How are you doing?"

The more he babbled, the more her grin broadened. Caleb huffed in the back. Stefan winced. A bear would sound more welcoming. The pretty lab tech chuckled.

"Someone didn't get the visit he hoped for..."

"Neve wanted to talk to our witness once more. She sent me in her place."

He followed as Lauren navigated between counters covered with test tubes and lab forms toward a large white board.

"Wow, you look busy."

"Tell me about it. Elections are coming and the administration is on the backs of all public services. The big boss is just freaking out. Roaring even more than usual. As if increasing statistics was going to make up for the scandal about the mayor's wife. Don't touch that, please."

Stefan instantly withdrew his hands from a microscope of some sort.

"Sorry. Who's on the grill now?"

Lauren picked up a report on the pile Caleb had just put down on a table and then discarded it.

"Ian Braich."

"Oops."

She raised an eyebrow, momentarily looking up from her notes, meeting with Stefan's impish grin.

"Not his lucky day, then…"

Caleb didn't look sorry at all.

"That's why he was more charming than usual earlier. So, who won that round? No, don't tell me. He was pissed, but not smug…"

Stefan bobbed his head.

"It was a close *ex aequo*."

Lauren unclipped a bunch of papers from her board with a devilish grin.

"One of these days, I'm going to put a bet on them…"

Caleb groaned in his microscope. Stefan's hands shot up.

"Hey, keep me out of it!"

"You're no fun. So, here you go."

He ogled at the columns and rows, unconvinced. When he turned to jump to the conclusions, Lauren hissed between her teeth.

"I *hate* saying that twice in a day, but I didn't find anything significant. The results are quite bizarre actually. See here?"

Stefan narrowed his eyes on a graph with weird shaped spikes.

"Hum, yes? What about it?"

"That's the X-ray result. We used it to verify if there was paint on your fragments, as well as their composition."

Stefan nodded, sensing the lecture coming.

"The spikes distribution on the graph and their size is related to the mineral content. Anyway, that's not the important part. The good news is that the samples are indeed painted porcelain. We noticed lead whites. And that's something, trust me, because the poor states of those samples–"

"We collected them the best we could. Between the firemen and the–"

"Yes, yes, I know. Don't interrupt me."

"Sorry… So what's the bad news?"

Lauren adjusted her glasses on the ridge of her nose. "Metal."

"But you said it was good to have lead…"

"Lead whites mark the pigment in the paint. I'm talking about metallic fragments." She tapped the tip of her finger on the graph. "In this particular case, those should not be here. Something's not right. And why is there so much sulfur? It can't be from the accelerant, the firemen would have noticed the change when they drenched the place, it would be in their report..." Lauren muttered to herself more than for Stefan's benefit. "No, something is definitely odd with this sample."

"Did you check another one?"

She glared above her glasses, obviously insulted by the question.

"Of course we did! We obtained more or less the same results with the dozen of fragments we tested. No, it's something else. I need more time. Caleb is scanning the most promising fragments now, so we'll try to assemble them to have an image."

"Wow, that would be great!"

Stefan sobered up almost immediately.

"How long will it take? I'm not sure the client will accept the delay…"

Lauren shrugged.

"This kind of puzzle is not going to solve itself overnight. I'd say about a week, maybe two."

"Oh."

In Lauren's alien timeframe, it probably meant three or four days. He sighed.

"I'll tell Neve. But you're sure there was a painting there, aren't you?"

Lauren waved impatiently.

"Yes, yes. My conclusions won't change because of the additional analysis, it's the support that—"

Stefan rolled the three pages report into a tube. The cute lab tech clasped her mouth shut, clearly unhappy with the treatment he gave her precious info.

"Fine. Now scoot. Caleb and I have work to do. We'll call you when we're done."

The named Caleb peered up from his microscope. Stefan took the cue. He pulled his zipper up, then down again when the fabric caught in the device. His next attempt had him elbowing the test tubes rack behind him. Lauren yelped. Caleb jumped to the rescue. The giant grabbed the rack right before the tubes fell off. Stefan offered his best puppy look.

"Oops… Sorry? I'll go now. Bye!"

Neither technician answered, though he heard a suspicious groan when the door banged behind him.

*

Neve closed her eyes and let her head roll backward on the header. The scent of furniture polish seemed to cling to her lungs, enhanced by every breath of cold air she took.

The only thing this trip to Connecticut had given her was the threat of a headache. The old hag had spent the whole time complaining about the insurance company delay. She didn't even seem to care about the items lost in the fire. But then, if the merry widow had banished her husband's collection to a warehouse, it wasn't out of love.

The young woman sighed, slightly angry with herself. Once more, she had overstepped her mandate, and wasted her time. Determining if the fire was an accident was the duty of the firefighters' department. Her role was limited to confirm if the most precious item on the insurance list, an 18th century tin-glazed porcelain plate from Delft, a Chinoiserie as the insurance contract described it, had indeed disappeared in the blaze. She was paid to collect whatever shard she could find, bring them to the lab for analysis, and provide the results; nothing more, nothing less. The job required her talents as an investigator, that was for sure...

She smiled bitterly, and turned the ignition. The migraine pulsing inside her skull started to sound a little too much like a certain police officer.

Chapter 3

Ian slumped into his chair, ignoring the mass of papers piled on his desk. His ears were still ringing from the captain's sermon. The man had no idea how loud his voice got when he started yelling for good. Not to mention he'd had more than his share today…

The young man opened his eyes again. Hoping that the paperwork would have magically disappeared was a wistful wish. He groaned. "I've got more pleasant thank you, even from you," Luke said as he put a cup in front of the tallest pile.

Ian jerked up. Fragrant whiffs swirled up to tickle his nose. The strong taste of almond exploded with the first sip. He clapped his tongue in pleasure.

"Right. Thanks for that."

Luke grinned, then pointed at the overloaded desk.

"I had a feeling you would need the boost. So, what did he want?"

The blond man stretched his arms in front of him, menacing the safety of the cup on the top of the closest stack of files. He grunted, "Bloody miracles. How come you escaped the lecture, anyway?"

Luke lowered himself to the chair facing Ian.

"Doc called me."

Ian instantly quit the bored act. He moved forward in his chair, eyes wide open, his hands linked between his knees. Luke nodded and opened the folder on his desk.

"Male Caucasian; five feet ten, probably in his late thirties or early forties–"

"Forty? He looked younger than I do! No way was this guy a tramp. You age quickly in the street."

"Doc said he won't confirm that until he has the epistemology and anthropology results."

Ian bumped his thumbs together as he registered the information.

"Right. Did he confirm the cause of the death?"

Luke flipped through the page toward the end of the report.

"Intense hypothermia. The weather report of the past week indicates that nights were cold. Maybe he was particularly sensitive to low temperatures."

"Very funny."

"Oh come on! This guy had his brain mushed by a .22, and you ask for the cause of death? Brighten up a little."

Ian grunted then reached backward to grab the toxicity report from the in-basket.

"Lauren said he probably drank and smoked stuff."

"You've got it, then. This guy weighed only around one hundred and fifty soaked to the bone. If he was robbed of his shoes early in the evening, the vasodilatation and the–"

Ian scowled.

"Your sense of humor is disastrous, and you're spending too much time with your sister."

Luke smirked. Ian picked up a pen to make it swirl between his fingers.

"Did you notice any bruises? Traces of a fight?"

"Nope."

The pen moved back and forth around his index finger. Luke read the rest of the report for himself, before putting the folder back on the desk and pushing it toward his partner.

"There are a couple of photos in there too."

Ian sneered.

"Just what I needed to bright up my day; death meat snapshots."

Luke glared back.

"Sarcasm's a vice, you know."

Ian didn't answer, focused on his cup of coffee and the documents before him.

Luke leaned back in his chair to look at his friend. Two and half years of partnership had taught him loads about the man behind the attitude and the golden-boy looks. Right now, energy was building up, close to the boiling point. He also knew that the stress was coming from his clashes of the day or the dead ends in their current investigation.

"Why don't you tell me what's wrong?"

The blond man glanced above his reading. His friend gave him a pointed look. Ian shrugged.

"Nothing. I'm fine."

"You've been torturing that pen for a good twenty minutes, and I'm starting to wonder why you bothered combing your hair this morning. Come on. What's on your mind?"

Ian threw the ballpoint away as if it had burnt him. His right hand shot up toward his nape, before he stopped midway in the air. He sighed.

"I... kind of..." he exhaled again, working his jaw left and right. "I pushed it a bit too far this morning, and I don't like it."

Surprised, Luke said, "Explain."

"She's so irritating! Can't have a bit of criticism without jumping up a man's throat. Anyway."

"You're talking about…"

"Neve. We ran into each other at the Bottom Stone."

Luke took back a mouthful of coffee.

"It can't be that bad. I can count on one hand the people you never argued with. You're not the most welcoming person."

A glare answered him.

"I don't make a habit of making women cry."

Luke lost his grip on the thankfully empty cup.

"You did what?"

Ian instantly switched into a defensive mode.

"She didn't burst into tears. Simply… She looked pretty shaken up."

"God, I can't let you out by yourself for even two hours. You know that Neve's associate and my sister…"

"Who on earth would want to date your sister?"

Ian shut up under Luke's darkening stare.

"Okay. Forget it."

"Call Neve and apologize; now," said Luke. A blank face answered him. Luke bobbed his head, and pushed on his feet. Ian Braich voicing out an apology was even less probable than seeing him admit he was wrong.

"Fine. Get up."

"I'm not going to–"

Luke interrupted the protest with a backflip of his hand.

"I promised Lauren to come give some self-defense tips at her kickboxing classes. You're coming with me."

Ian sulked.

"Out of the question. Your promise, your problem. Why can't Lauren use the police training facilities anyway?"

"And spend more time with a grumpy head like yourself? Even I have my doubts sometimes! Grab your stuff, we're late."

Ian's scornful look got lost in Luke's back.

*

As usual, Neve stopped grouching as soon as she started undressing to change into her yoga pants and tee-shirt. Stefan had coerced her into coming to the gym, officially because she needed the workout, and unofficially because he wanted the support while he (finally) invited Lauren for a drink. Thinking of it, a good sweat and Stefan's clumsy flirting was exactly what she needed to clear her mind.

The place was one of the best-kept secrets in town. Only a few people knew the old tobacco warehouse had been converted into an ultra-modern training facility. The architects had managed to preserve the charm of the nineteenth-century building. In daylight, the sun was pouring in through the numerous square windows to set the brick walls aflame. At night, bare bulb pendant lights supervised the trainers. The same old tarnish prevailed in the locker rooms. Copper piping and porcelain tiles gleamed in the lockers. The staff kept towels and other supplies on painted pine shelves.

Neve whistled discreetly between her teeth when she stepped into the main room. Even by New-Year's-Eve resolution standards, the place was packed. People were gritting their teeth while cycling. Groans escorted the oval of cross-trainers. Even the steppers were taken. On the other side of the room, the spek and Bowflex machines worked in tandem, one person waiting while the other completed her circuit. She guessed the stretching room was just as cramped.

More people stood near the room where Stefan's kickboxing class was about to begin. She spotted him with two men and a dark ponytail she guessed was Lauren. Neve waved, but her friend was absorbed in his conversation and didn't return the gesture.

The young woman circled a threesome of giggling girls to access the water fountain and refill her bottle. Her gaze screened the room once more. Hopefully, the kickboxing class would clear the room a little, so a machine or two became available.

Her eyes stopped on a rower, in front of the treadmills. The man almost had the device jumping backward with each too-vigorous pull. Sweat plastered his dark blue T-shirt between his shoulder blades. She couldn't see his face, but his neck and hips were tensed in effort. Neve imagined a strong clenched jaw, and darkened eyes focused on the screen in front of him. She wet her lips without thinking. The masculine shoulders rose in rhythm with his rowing, but his back jolted in brief, sharp rasps. Unable to resist, she corked her bottle closed, and moved toward the man. If he wasn't done, at least she would manage to take a glimpse at his face while filling the reservation form. A girl could dream...

"Excuse me, are you–" Neve's jaw fell "Oh, I can't believe it!"

Ian dropped the handle. The heavy bar banged against the central axle. Ian tried to grab it back before it hit the monitor set above the caster wheel. He missed. His hand got caught under the chain while it rolled itself up. Ian hissed in pain.

Neve crouched instinctively.

"Let me see."

He pulled it out with a loud, "Back off."

Shocked by the rebuff, she jumped back on her feet.

"Can you be more obnoxious? I just–"

"Problem here?"

Stefan and the kickboxing trainer appeared behind her back. Neve clammed up. Ian untangled his large frame from the rower, massaging his hand while towering above them all.

"No."

By the look on Stefan's face, her grimace was not exactly welcoming.

"You know the rules, Neve. All fighting for an apparatus is to be solved in the ring."

Ian backed away, nearly bumping into the treadmill.

"I am not–"

"Ah, yes, absolutely!"

The blond policeman swallowed in shock. She couldn't really want to box with him. Her head barely reached his chin, for Christ's sake! Was she completely mad? He took another step backward, pointing at the classroom over his shoulder.

"Luke enlisted my help for the self-defense class, so I'll just–"

"Just in case you didn't notice, he's doing just fine without you. This way, if you please..."

Neve's smug invite screeched on his nerves. He grunted between clenched teeth, and followed.

The ring was more a set of mattresses arranged together on the floor than a real arena. Neve opened a chest and pulled out two padded sticks. He caught the one she threw in his direction in midair. He huffed.

"You should put on protection."

"I don't need any. But maybe you'll want to protect some vital parts?"

Ian made the baton swirl in his hand, testing its weight. He glared.

"No hit below the belt, or to the head."

"Stop talking and fight, Braich."

She launched the first attack in the same breath. The cushioned end aimed for his shoulder. He avoided the blow by an inch. The stick felt strange in his hands. Ian adjusted his grasp on the weapon, shoving her away. Neve chuckled.

"What is it, officer? Your mother taught you not to hit a woman, even with a flower?"

"That's 'detective,' and I strongly suggest you shut up about my family."

Ian sucked air in. She was trying to rile him so he rushed into her mad scheme without thinking. No way in hell was he going to indulge her. He lowered his guard.

"I'm not playing this game."

"As you wish!"

Neve jumped toward him again. This time, she moved left and right in fast quick jabs. Ian straightened up his stick to deflect the blows raining on him, without success. The little she-devil was damned serious! He grunted each time she brushed his shoulders. Neve darted left again. He was too slow, and she punched his arm hard. Her grin grew in pleasure.

"Your defense is sloppy."

Ian steadied his stance with one foot behind him. He still hesitated to give their exchange his full attention. She was quick on her feet, and strong for a woman her size. But he was taller and more powerful. If he did as she asked, she could get seriously hurt. Her next attack on his right side deviated as he pivoted on his heel. The movement left her back unprotected. Unable to resist, he tapped her buttocks lightly with the cushioned end of his stick.

"Getting tired, sweetheart?"

Neve glowered. She tightened her grip, stepping away from him to circle his spot like a cat which had just been splashed by water. Ian followed her movements, careful not to cross his feet and offer her an occasion to throw him down. He longed to pick up her challenge. His fingers flexed on the fake battle stick.

"Remember, you asked for this."

She smirked at the bravado. Ian struck the upper end of her stick hard. Neve backed under the force. He pushed his advantage. He tried to slip his weapon under hers to disarm her. She jumped sideways. He managed to tap the small of her back again.

This time, she snarled. Ian refrained the need to jest, now totally focused on their fight. The baton moved easily between his hands, more familiar by the minute. Her hand moved down her own weapon, until both hands held it like a club, or a sword. Ian narrowed his eyes, following the constant motion she imprinted to her stick. Neve lunged. Ian blocked the slash targeting his left side at the last second.

"I didn't know you were left-handed."

Neve huffed, "There's a lot you don't know about me!"

She spun on her heels so fast he nearly missed her next move. Her baton flew into her right hand, then toward his head. Ian dodged. Then the stick changed sides again and he had to stomp his stick into the mattress to keep his footing. Neve used the momentum to kick it away. Ian tottered sideways. His knees cracked in protest when he pushed upward.

Surprised, Neve stopped, eyeing her opponent with a mix of surprise and guilt. Ian lurched. He grabbed Neve's stick, making her whirl. Her own baton squeezed against her throat, while he pressed her back into her chest. His breath tickled her cheek.

"Got you."

She wriggled to escape, to no avail. The young woman gasped. Ian released the pressure by an inch. Her foot stomped between his. He felt her brace herself, the tension grazing his chest. Her shoulder moved sideways against his collarbone. Ian instantly crouched to counter the motion with his heavier weight, but too late. Before he knew it, he was lying on his back. The stick was now forced down his own neck, his palms still wrapped against the cushioned ends. Neve's knee pressed the sensitive muscle under his ribcage. She grinned.

"I won."

Ian slitted his eyes. She was panting, and a curl had escaped her ponytail to brush his T-shirt. Her eyes sparkled with pleasure. Her arms trembled in the effort to maintain the pose. She didn't give him time to decide if he wanted to use force and reverse their position. She stood gracefully and arranged her hair as if nothing had happened.

"Thanks for the warm-up. The loser cleans the mess, by the way."

Ian straightened up, ankles crossed before him and his hands linked around his bent knees. He twisted his neck to ease the kink growing there. Looking around, he saw Luke still occupied with his groupies in the classroom. The whole exchange had probably just taken ten or fifteen minutes. He sighed, and resigned himself to wait.

Chapter 4

Neve rested her hips against the counter for a closer look in the mirror. She traced the still tender flesh with her finger and winced. After two days, the euphoria of pinning Ian Braich's damned ego to the ground had faded, undermined by the discovery of the mark on her arm and a nasty feeling he had let her win.

The bruise blossomed in greenish purple, though. All things considered, she was glad he hadn't put his whole mind to the fight. She would have ended up beaten black and blue.

"Evy?"

"Hold on a second!"

She dropped her sleeve and picked up her hairbrush. Stefan peered inside half a minute later.

"Lauren is here."

She looked puzzled for a second then returned to brushing the tip of her ponytail.

"Ah, yes, she's picking you up. I'll be there in a minute."

Her friend bent his head sideways.

"What's the matter?"

"Nothing, I'm fine."

She smiled at him in the mirror. A strand of hair curled around her brush. Stefan said, "You should come with us. We could call Caleb, I'm sure he w–"

"Yes, I'm sure he does... But I don't. So thanks, but no. Besides, I have plans."

Stefan shot her a suspicious stare.

"You're not going to work, are you?"

Neve grabbed him by the shoulders, pushing him in front of her as they left her bedroom. He resisted as she shoved him forward. She grumbled.

"No, I'm not going to work. I'm just going to crawl on the sofa with the remote control, potato chips or maybe popcorn, and indulge in a *Game of Thrones* marathon. Now move."

He still didn't look convinced. Neve eyed Lauren standing near the indoor stairs. The petite brunette shot them a curious look, as if she were observing some particular specimen under her microscope. Neve sneered up her sleeve. Even if she couldn't persuade her best friend that she needed the me-time, she could still pull at a few strings.

Neve angled her head to murmur under her breath, "If you keep going on like that, Lauren is going to think you are afraid to stay alone with her."

He pouted. *Almost there.* Neve added, "Or she might think you changed your mind."

This blow hit. Stefan straightened up at once, nearly causing her to lose her footing. He hissed, "You're not funny" before turning puppy eyes on his date.

"Sorry; there was a *huge* spider in the bathroom, and Neve is such a girl when it comes to those..."

Neve rolled her eyes at the lie. Lauren smirked, visibly not buying a word of it.

"Aren't we all? Are you sure you don't want to join us, Neve? That spider could have friends..."

It was all she could do not to groan. Was it so hard to believe she wanted to spend her Friday night by herself for once, rolled up in a coverlet with flannel pajamas on in front of the TV? She liked the funky forensic, she really did, but if Lauren also mentioned her co-worker, she was going to scream. Neve crossed her arms over her chest, one delicate eyebrow crooked up.

"Really, you're asking me to choose between a noisy, crowded, smelly pub and John Snow?"

Stefan grumbled, "Not that smelly…"

Lauren hooked one arm around her date's waist.

"At least we tried. Let's go, Stefan."

The young man jerked when she squeezed his hip lightly. Neve laughed up her sleeve. Maybe Stefan was a bit scared after all. She waved at the leaving couple. "Have fun!"

She waited for the door to close. Right before the clang, Lauren's voice echoed from the bottom of the stairs.

"Oh, by the way, Neve, I'm still waiting for a couple of results but I sent you a preliminary version of my report. You might find it interesting!"

The young woman snorted. Trust Lauren not to leave the last word to anyone.

*

On the screen, armies clashed in roar and thunder. Neve shifted to rest on her other side. The fall of kings went barely noticed. She winced when her upper arm pressed into the seat and moved again. She'd been playing that game for about two hours, turning and thrashing to find a comfortable position. Laying down, sitting up, propping her feet up on the coffee table, nothing worked. She just couldn't do it. Exasperated, she welcomed the credits and leaped to her feet for another trip to the fridge.

Her fiftieth attempt came up empty-handed. She didn't feel like nibbling any more than staying quietly in front of the TV.

Neve slumped back on the couch, annoyed. Damned Stefan, Lauren, and their allusions. She hadn't planned to work. She didn't *want* to work. What she wanted was to nestle on the couch, and watch whatever G.R.R. Martin and HBO had planned for her favorite characters.

She snorted. All right, so maybe that was not all she wanted. She conceded she was curious. It didn't mean she was going to jump on her email and read that report until her eyes bled.

Neve grabbed a cushion, focusing on the flat screen once more. By the time the opening sneak peek ended, she was wriggling again, folding and unfolding her legs from under her.

She glared at the corner behind the couch. Her laptop pouch was squeezed between the storage bench and an owl-shaped ceramic umbrella pot Stefan had convinced her to buy at a yard sale last summer. She gritted her teeth. The white thing was ugly. They didn't use umbrellas for God's sake!

The cushion crashed in the stairs. She blew some air out her nose. Her sore arm protested when a second projectile fell short too.

"You're useless, Neve. Not even able to hit a stupid sitting bird ten feet from you with a damned pillow!"

With another groan, she got up to gather her ammunitions.

The shrill jarred her nerves. Neve jumped to attention, pillows in hand, ready to fight. The noise grew in volume. She kicked herself out loud.

"Just the phone, you dimwit. Hello? Hello?"

The line went dead. Neve scowled at the ID on the screen.

"Not this again…"

This was the third time this month that she received a phone call from the ECV Central which handled the agency's security system. The first two had been false alarms. The building was old, and one of the windows unclenched when the wind gushed hard. But Stefan had fixed it. Or rather, Stefan had said he would talk to Terence, so the janitor changed the window sash lock. It'd been polar cold all week long. Maybe the repair was delayed, and he forgot to tell her about it?

She punched the reply button. Even if it was a false alarm, the central should have rung until she'd picked up the call. They were supposed to, unless the alarm stopped within the first thirty seconds after firing up.

"Heaven Safe Security?… Hi, Neve Lass speaking. I just received a phone call from your ECV… Yes, please, patch me through to the central…"

Terence had a passkey. If he hadn't repaired the window like he was supposed to, and the alarm went off, then…

"Yes, I'm here. Neve Lass from GLPI. Did the alarm go off at the office?… I received a call from the central… Well, I *would* know if your operator had waited until I picked up the phone… I'm not complaining, I want to know if the alarm fired up… Yes, Neve Lass from GLPI. My ID is…"

Neve pinched the bridge of her nose while she recited the 7-digit code.

"Yes, I'm waiting…"

For an emergency service, they were all but in a hurry. She wanted to scream. A solid minute later, she was on the verge of kicking the coffee table in front of her. Finally, the operator came back on line.

"… If I want you to check why the system suddenly went silent? Yes, I would like you to check." She could barely believe they asked. "Yes, please, please call me back…. Yes, you can call this number."

The line went dead, which was just as well. It was all she could do to stay polite. The young woman threw her legs off the couch. If you want a thing done well, do it yourself.

*

The snow crunched under her foot when she stepped on the sidewalk. Neve shivered. The night was so cold her jaw hurt when she clenched her teeth to stop their chattering. The thin yoga pants she wore did little to keep the chilly wind at bay. She pulled the zipper of her parka up. Her hands hurt when she pushed them deep in her pockets. It seemed it had stopped snowing only for the temperature to drop. The occasional cars grumbled painfully as they skidded by. Even the street lamps gave the impression they had to fight to stay alive. At least she didn't have far to go.

Her wool gloves slipped on the metal, wet from the occasional flurries that danced down from the roofs. She grabbed the knob through her sleeve. This time, she managed to yank the door open. Her lungs almost squinted in shock when the warmer air replaced the outside chill.

A ghostly glow peered through the fogged glass. She suspected the crystalline crescent carved on the window was ice. Neve inhaled carefully. The warmer air rasped the back of her throat. Usually, she loved the special smell of old building, a mix of floor wax and dust. Right now, the odor caught her in a vicious grip. She wheezed, "Terence? Mr. Whale?"

Her croak reverberated on the walls. The hall was empty, the Irish caretaker out of sight. If he had shut off the alarm, he had already retreated to his apartment at the end of the hall.

"Terence? Are you in?"

Neve debated whether to insist. Terence Whale was a lonely man with a bottomless –and eclectic– passion for words. If she knocked on his door now, she risked drowning in an ocean ruled by Yeats, James Joyce and David Bowie. She would never muster the energy to go up if she visited him first. She turned toward the stairs.

The dark wooden floor squawked when she moved forward. Neve fumbled for the light switch. The old timer button creaked a little when she turned it. Usually the cackling sound it made clucking down was charming. Right now, it screeched on her nerves.

Slowly, the filament paled until a weak yellow circle crowned the bulb. She released a breath, only to stiffen when the gold light reddened and waved. The bubbly bloom shrank as if it was about to die.

A trickle of melted snow chafed the skin of her neck. She didn't want to climb the spiral staircase in the dark. The used carpet held into place by even older braces was treacherous enough in daylight. She had lost count of how many times Stefan had lost his footing and hit the copper edge that armed the planks. All right, maybe his habit of hopping two steps at a time didn't help, but still. The glow wobbled painfully.

"Come on…"

The light flickered, once, twice, then it dilated again and seemed to steady itself.

Her hand clasped around the banister, Neve began to climb.

Chapter 5

Ian selected a peanut at random and popped it into his mouth, his attention focused on the screen. The video clip unfolded its psychedelic colors in some rhythm he couldn't hear, as the flow of conversations and laugher drowned the music. He didn't really mind, though he wished the constant noise tuned down a bit. The clatter seemed to reverberate down his neck to that kink at the junction with his shoulder blade he was unable to get rid of, no matter how many times he stretched or rolled his shoulder.

It had been a long day on top of an even longer week. The John Doe case was going nowhere. His eyes crossed from hours on the disappearance list, with no results so far. He had welcomed Luke's suggestion of a night out with open arms. Now, confronted with the bar's reality, he started to regret it.

"Anything to drink, handsome?"

He glanced at the waitress. She was pretty, in a sassy sort of way, coral pink lips and smoky eyes. Her short black skirt showed off slim legs. In comparison, her neckline was designed to make Pamela Anderson jealous. Not exactly his type, but not far from it either. If he had been in the mood, he would probably have answered the tease and played back, to see how far she was willing to push the game. She looked at him expectantly. Ian shook his head, pointing toward the bar.

"My partner is taking care of it, thanks."

Shock flashed on her face, before she caught herself and smiled.

"Sure. Let me know if you change your mind, okay?"

He backed on his seat, for once happy with the misunderstanding. He wasn't fit for the chasing game tonight. And he preferred to be the cat rather than the mouse anyway.

"Here you go. What's so funny?"

"Nothing. Just a slip of the tongue that goes my way, for once."

Luke frowned, then shrugged as Ian rose a self-explanatory eyebrow. His friend grinned, grabbing a couple of peanuts.

"Good thing we're not here for the ladies, eh?"

Ian sampled his beer. The amber liquid sizzled on his tongue, bringing a rich, sweet taste, which he compared with caramel. Not bad, especially with the salty peanuts.

"I would ask why you chose this particular place, but I saw Lauren came in minutes ago."

Luke's head twisted toward the bar. Ian took another sip.

"They took a booth near the lounge; on your right."

This time, Luke turned carefully to scan the crowd in the approximate direction of the cocktail area. His brows furrowed when he failed to spot the familiar silhouette he was looking for. He sat back in his booth, frowning. Ian chuckled.

"You're so screwed... She's going to bite your head off if she finds us."

Luke focused on his own drink. Ian asked, "I thought you liked the guy, anyway, why–"

"I do," Luke groaned. "It doesn't mean I won't check him out. She's my baby sister."

"I have a sister, and I never felt compelled to stalk her."

"I'm not stalking–"

"Really? And what do you call it then? Good evening, Ian."

The blond man nodded quickly and dove on his bock. Lauren darted murderous eyes on her brother, arms crossed over her chest. He guessed her foot was one breath away from stomping.

"So?"

"Hi… You look great…"

The compliment thinned and vanished as soon as Luke noticed his sheepish act didn't mollify her. Luke scratched the side of his glass with his thumb, eyeing Ian from under his lashes, begging for help. One stiletto tapped slightly on the floor. He gave in. But if he was to go down, he would not go alone… Luke pointed at Ian.

"I had to distract this guy here, before he–"

"Excuse me, but I'm pretty sure *Ian* chose *this* particular place to hang out."

Ian preferred to keep his mouth shut. The feisty brunette glared. It was kind of funny to see how small their difference of height and strength was, all a sudden. Not that he was going to point that out.

"Well…"

"Oh, shut up. I can't believe you're still doing this. In high school, it was already insufferable. We're grown up now, remember? I *teach* self-defense classes for God's sake. And Stefan… If it were Gil, it would already be too much, but Stefan!"

"Who's Gil?"

"This is not the point!"

Her voice shrilled. Ian tightened his grip on his glass. It felt as if her frustration pulled every nerve connected to those stress knots in his upper back.

"Hi guys."

Stefan gave a quick smile at Lauren when she slipped her arm under his.

"Ah, Stefan, here you are. Well, *dear brother*, it was nice seeing you but–"

"Huh…"

Ian lifted his eyes toward the embarrassed new-comer. Lauren's frown narrowed on him. Ill-at-ease, Stefan jittered.

"I… The call, you know, that was the ECV because I'm second in line. They can't reach Neve but they talked to her before and–"

"Stefan, you're not making sense. Take a deep breath and start again."

Lauren glared at her brother for his intrusion. The advice did work, however.

"Right. Apparently, the alarm at the office set off again and stopped. It's the third time this month. The central called Neve, and they were supposed to get in touch as soon as they knew why, but she's not picking up the call."

"So?"

Lauren interfered before Stefan could argue. She sounded more accommodating than before. Ian wondered if she was just resigned to the fact her date was going down, fast.

"Maybe she went to the office and forgot her cell?"

Stefan shook his head.

"No, that's not like her."

Luke stood.

"Let's go and check, then."

This time, it was Ian's turn to scowl.

"You're overreacting. Lauren's right; she probably forgot her phone, or she went to bed.

Stefan turned to Ian.

"You don't know Neve. If she says she expects to hear from you, she means it. You're better to call, trust me." He gave a puppy look to the brunette. "I'm worried."

Lauren pursed her lips then said, "All right; Stefan, you're going with Ian. I'm following with Luke, we have a discussion to finish."

Her brother opened his mouth to protest, but she had already spun on her heels. Luke jumped on his feet to follow. Stefan looked sheepish.

"Sorry…"

Ian blew on the hair falling in his eyes noisily.

"Right. Come on."

*

The car skirted between snow thrower trucks and iced benches, Ian's driving somehow impacted by his jittery co-pilot. At least Stefan didn't mix up his lefts and rights, so besides avoiding snow drifts and orange warning lights, it was an easy, if not comfortable ride.

Stefan put his phone down.

"Still no answer. Turn left at the next crossing, then straight and right at the end of the street. We're on Harmon's."

Ian flashed to signal Luke and pumped on the brakes.

"I'm sure she's fine. Probably engrossed in something."

His passenger shot him a doubtful smile and shrugged. His eyes were scanning the small screen again. Ian focused on the white blanket in front of him. Half an hour ago, he had a bock of beer in hands and wondered if the coming waitress was worth the effort. Well, he had, for at least a couple of seconds. Anyway, now he was set

39

on a different chase, the results of which promised to be far less pleasing. He grouched, "I can just imagine how happy your boss is going to be when you break into her room."

No way was he walking in first, cop or not. He swore the tension in his neck had started with their sparing session at the gym.

"Can we put on the blue lights?"

"I don't think it's necessary."

A police car and an ambulance damped the street in blue, yellow and red. Ian parked on the other side and cut the engine. Stefan bolted out of the car toward the open door.

"Neve!"

"Sir, you can't..."

Ian flashed his shield.

"Detective Braich, Division 219. What happened here?"

The uniform who had tried to stop Stefan bowed his head at him.

"Emergency call, sir. Potential 459. We–"

"Get rid of this idiotic mask, young man. I'm perfectly able to breathe on my own. I'm telling you I'm fine! I was born during the first raids on London in December 1940 so don't think a little fall is going to bring me down. Scoot!"

The paramedic rolled his eyes at a man in his seventies with peppered hair and a bushy moustache who struggled to escape his attentions. Ian strolled toward him, Luke and Lauren on his tail. Pale blue eyes carried over them to stop on him.

"You. You look more capable than this lot. I'm Terence Whale. I'm the caretaker. Can you please explain to those *gentlemen* that maybe someone upstairs requires their attention more than I do?"

"The second medic already went up, Sir. Hey! You! No closer!"

Ian frowned at the rookie who sprinted – skidded – toward the back of the police car to shove a curious bystander away. Terence Whale clasped his tongue, his moustache shivering in satisfaction.

"Good. They need someone in charge. Youth tends to run around like a headless chicken. You want to know what happened, I suppose?"

Ian did his best not to smile at the pompous tone. He settled for a quick motion of the hand. Stefan was nowhere to be seen. Lauren was all ears. Terence nodded to himself, and cleared his throat.

"I thought so. Well, that's simple. The alarm at GLPI – that's Miss Neve's office – set off then it stopped. I didn't think much of it at first; there's a window there that needs some repairs, and with that wind…" The old man slapped the hand of the medic who was trying to take his pulse. "I said enough, you. Anyway; I was reading, and then I heard stomping and scratching, as if two people were fighting above my living-room. I didn't hesitate. I called 9-1-1 and I got out of my apartment to investigate but then some oaf knocked the wind out of me."

"He fell in the stairs…"

The second intervention from the rookie had as little success as the previous one.

"Anyhow–"

Ian cut him off.

"Thank you, Mr. Whale. Please go with our paramedic so he can complete his own report."

The moustache quivered once more, but the old man complied. Ian waved at Luke, and they entered the building. Suddenly he regretted not taking Stefan at his word. They might have reached the place sooner.

41

Five minutes later, he wondered why he had even bothered.

RECKLESS ILLUSIONS

Chapter 6

"I'm all right, thank you."

The paramedic shook his head.

"What is it with you all tonight? I'll be downstairs if you change your mind."

Stefan gave him an apologetic smile. Ian snorted.

"You're acting like a child."

He turned his attention back to the desk, picking up a binder.

"Hey! Don't mess with my things! I'll handle it!"

Neve grimaced as she stood to face the detective. Her strained neck hurt like mad. Stefan and Lauren exchanged a knowing look. Ian's expression mirrored Neve's customary pout to a fault. He caught their amused gazes, and instantly changed his posture, hands crossed at his back, shoulders square. He glowered toward the unyielding woman.

"You can't investigate your own case."

Her voice dripped with ice.

"I don't see why not."

"You're emotionally involved. It messes with your judgment. All the good investigators know when to step back."

"I'm not a good investigator, you repeat that often enough," Neve challenged while she poked a finger his chest. Moving made her head throb. She bit the inner side of her cheek in hopes the pain would keep her head clear. The world darkened; her vision narrowed into a blur. She ignored it. Neve hung upon the last crumbles of her strength to stay upright.

"I'll do as I please."

If thoughts could kill, he would be strangling her.

"This is a police affair. Don't get in my way or I–"

"It's not if I don't press charges."

"Well I do!"

Both opponents turned to Stefan, one with a satisfied sneer, the other painfully incredulous.

"Stefan!"

"You won't have it your way this time, Neve. Ian," he pointed at the supplies scattered on the floor, "someone stole my lucky pen. I want the police to open a case for robbery."

Stefan glimpsed at his best friend. A bruise started to mar the base of her neck.

"And add assault to the charge."

Ian nodded with a sly grin.

"Yes, Sir. I'll need a description of that pen."

"I have pictures."

Neve whimpered. In pain or desperation for their stupid exchange, neither man could tell. She wobbled back to the couch to slouch down on the cushions. Stefan joined her in two strides.

"Neve?"

"M'all right. Just a little tired…"

The incessant ballet around the room hammered inside her skull. The multicolor flashes pouring from the windows were the worst. They exploded like angry St-Elmo's fires so her stomach mistook the room for a lifeboat in the storm. A feminine hand grabbed her chin to lift it. Neve stifled a moan. Her pupils hurt when they tried to accommodate under the brutish glare Lauren swayed before her.

"She may have a concussion. Luke, call the medic back."

Neve fumbled with her shirt, her breathing labored by the pain. Her words slurred.

"I don't need… an ambulance. M 'kay."

The world reeled, then steadied again.

"I'll take her home, Lauren. Hospitals, they're not her thing."

"Stop spea– speaking as if I wasn't… in the room."

"Sorry, Evy. Can you stand up?"

Ian looked away. If he hadn't been so focused on helping Neve up, Stefan would have sworn he was blushing. Meanwhile Lauren fired instructions.

"Give her aspirin. Let her sleep if she wants to, but wake her up every thirty minutes for the first two hours, then every hour. If she complains she's in pain, she retches, or her eyes don't react to light, call 9-1-1."

Ian eyed the exchange as Stefan nodded less and less vigorously under the storm of instructions. Lauren noticed too.

"On your way down, please talk to that friend of yours, would you, Stefan? What's his name, Lawrence?"

"Terence."

"Right. Terence. He refused to go to the hospital until he was sure Neve's fine. For a man his age, falling down the stairs can be quite dangerous."

Luke and Ian exchanged a frown. Neve lifted her head slowly.

"Terence… fell?"

Stefan caught the ball.

"Yes. You know how he feels about the American medical system. Didn't want to hear the first thing about going to the hospital. But maybe if you set an example…"

This time, Neve didn't protest. Ian couldn't retain a grin. Lauren and Stefan had outmaneuvered her without a sweat.

Ian watched their silhouettes move away out of the corner of his eyes, a bitter taste in his mouth. Besides, if he stayed ogling at the strange couple, he would probably say something he'd regret later.

He disapproved of PIs. Neve was a particularly frustrating specimen. It didn't mean he wished her harm. Her stumble didn't fit. Where was the irritating female who tried to beat the crap out of him with a stick only days before? Stefan kept her close, so that her head rested on his shoulder. Ian scratched his skull.

"They'll be fine, Ian. The night team will be here shortly. I'll just head home now," Lauren said.

His growl came out between clenched teeth.

"If you think you can leave, then leave."

Lauren stifled a chuckle, unconcerned about the storm brewing in Ian's glare.

"Down, boy; I bred them well. Just stop making them squirm, or they'll miss something, and then I'll be very, very unhappy."

She arranged her coat and scarf, then blew a kiss to her brother and left.

The blond detective huffed toward his partner.

"Your sister is impossible."

"So I've been told…"

*

The light spread out of the wrong side of the bed. Neve rubbed at her lashes to chase the itchy sensation, before she opened her eyes slowly. She blinked a few times to get accustomed to the callous glare.

Her tongue was parched. She spotted water in a baby jug on the plastic table to her left. The mattress protector whined when she reached for the bottle. Neve squirmed to get comfortable against the pillow and then sipped her water while her brain connected the dots.

Things were still a bit confused, but she remembered being knocked out by a shadow, and waking up to be yelled at by a Neanderthal who called himself a detective. Then Stefan had outfoxed her into climbing in the ambulance with Terence. So now she was alone in a hospital room that stank from chemicals, with a stupid backless blouse on.

"Hi, Sleeping Beauty. How are you feeling?"

"Betrayed. What time is it?"

Stefan put his load on the empty bed beside hers and leaned to kiss the crown of her head, ignoring her scowl.

"A little after noon. Doc said your scanner looked okay, so the nurse gave you a little something to sleep. Wished I could have had the same, since you went out in a blink."

Neve gazed at her friend. His eyes were deep in their sockets, making his high cheekbones even more prominent. Feeling a little bad for her dry welcome, she offered a tiny smile.

"Is there a chance for decent clothes in there?"

"Maybe… Can I watch as you get up?"

"I have panties on, Stefan."

She flushed a deep red. He grinned from ear to ear.

"Spoil sport. All right, I suppose it means you're okay."

The relief in his voice added to her guilt. He really did look tired. Neve patted the bed. Stefan obeyed and nestled against her side. They stayed quiet for a while, listening to the hospital's buzz.

"Sorry I scared you."

"That you did. You also ruined my date."

Neve smiled.

"Does having Braich handling the investigation settle the score?"

"Nope. You owe me, big time."

"I'll make diner."

She nodded.

"And the dishes. For a week."

"Deal. Can I get up now?"

Stefan jumped on his feet.

"Okay. I'll check you out."

Neve waited until the door closed to push the thin cover away and test her legs. She jolted a little when her bare feet touched the cold tiles. Her knees felt like rubber. Her head was a little heavy on her shoulders and her back was stiff, but besides that, she was fine. The headache and nausea of the previous night were gone. Which meant she was ready to confront that idiot of Ian. A chill ran down her spine. As soon as she had some real clothes on, that is.

*

Lauren entered the small kitchen with her hands pushed deep in her lab coat. Luke looked up from his cup of coffee.

"Hey, what's up? I thought you were off duty this weekend?"

"I am. But with what happened yesterday, I wanted to complete the analyses on Neve's case. Who knows, maybe it relates to her assault."

The brunette sat on the chair next to his, lost in thought. Her stare lingered on his cup long enough for Luke to take the hint. He got to his feet and grabbed the pot of coffee to pour her some.

"What does she work on?"

"I don't have all the details. She gave me some fragments to identify. Do you know what the problem is between them?"

"Between who?"

Lauren played her nails on the side of her mug.

"Don't play dumb. Ian and Neve. They can't be in the same room for more than two minutes without getting at each other's throat. What's the story? Did he break her heart?"

Ian butted in, "Why do you suppose it is my fault?"

Luke buried his nose in his coffee. Lauren took in the familiar frown, cutting tone included.

"Feminine support, dear. It's always the guy's fault. So, what is it? You had a hot steaming affair that ended in an epic fail?"

Ian crook an eyebrow, amused. His eyes stayed icy.

"Wouldn't you like to know."

Lauren pushed to her feet. She tapped his shoulder in passing.

"I'll know, even if I have to tear the truth out of you… Oh, by the way, Neve checked out of the hospital after lunch. Stefan said he's caging her in for the day, but will consider well intentioned visitors tomorrow. See you later…"

The door flipped behind her. Ian turned to his partner.

"Did I mention she's impossible?"

Luke nodded.

"Once or twice. But she has a point though. You're acting weird around Neve. I mean, even for you, being that aggressive is out of character."

"I don't like amateurism."

Ian's snarl met with patient dark eyes. He didn't want to speak about Neve, or how she reminded him of gloomier days, when even tiptoeing around his parents' house was too noisy. Luke sampled his coffee without a word, waiting.

"It's personal."

"Okay. She's off-limits. Got it."

"I didn't say... Hell, think what you want, I don't care. Can we go to work now? We still have 193 files to check for our John Doe."

Luke grunted.

"I thought you had gone through the whole bunch with the visual recognition software yesterday?"

"I did. Those came in this morning, fresh from Immigration."

"You've got to be kidding me..."

"Do I look like I'm kidding?"

The linoleum squealed as they pushed their chairs to stand. Lauren quickly padded away from the door toward the stairs and her lab. If even her brother –and Ian's self-appointed best friend- didn't know about his secret, then it was definitely worth digging up.

*

Neve wanted to go and give her statement, but Stefan didn't have the same urgency to go and meet with the police. He insisted on going back home so she could have some rest *'I slept all morning!'* and eat *'We can have a bite at the Stone'*. Every argument met a deaf ear. She knew him well enough to know that once he was set on something, he wouldn't budge. So Neve resigned herself to be pampered for the rest of the day.

Her roommate refused to give her anything more tiring than sitting on the couch. She was deprived of her computer, of her cell phone, and if she hadn't threatened him of bodily harm him, he would probably have stripped her of the TV remote control as well. Finally, they agreed on an Action/Adventure comedy they had seen about a hundred times, and huddled together under the blanket. It didn't take much time before Bruce Willis and Danny Aiello lulled them both into sleep.

Chapter 7

The door was little more than a dark rectangle. The trembling bulb had died out while she was midway up the steps. A pale glow dribbled from the sole window then waned in the shadows inches from the frosted glass.

Neve hesitated on the threshold. The night was black on black. Had they shut the store before leaving for the day? She didn't remember. There was a switch on the left side. Once she'd opened the door...

Neve awoke with a start. She blinked to chase away the swirling colors before her eyes, then straightened up awkwardly. Stefan grumbled in his sleep then buried his face in the cushions. She extracted herself from the blanket, grateful for the lamp they had lit earlier. Her forehead and the back of her throat burned. Her heart steadied though the punch at her ribs still hurt. She waited an instant before pushing onto her feet. The world remained more or less clear. Satisfied, Neve padded toward the sink for a glass of water.

The clock on the stove confirmed it was past 6 p.m. The glass emptied too quickly to calm her thirst. Neve shivered. *That's just an effect of the painkiller*, she thought. Her body seemed caught between daze and alertness. She swallowed more water, almost glad for the sharp taste in her mouth. Stefan snored lightly. At least one of them was resting.

The nightmare lurked in the back of her mind. No, not a nightmare, a memory; she *had* fumbled with her keys. Considering, finding the hole in the dark had been pretty easy. She remembered pushing the door, poking inside to find the lights and then…

Neve brushed the tip of her fingers on the base of her skull and winced.

"Huh, whatyoudoing?" Stefan asked groggily. His hair spiked in very strange directions. He blinked like an owl. Neve held up her glass with a smile.

"I was thirsty. Want some?"

"Nah… Think the phone's ringing…"

"What phone?"

She didn't hear a thing.

"Tso'kay… Have it…"

Stefan sank back in the couch, dead to the world once again. Neve smiled. Her eyes fluttered, as if suddenly she couldn't keep them open. Less than a minute later, she was tucked in bed, and fast asleep again. The laptop she had picked up to check her email stayed unlit next to her.

*

"What do we have?"

The room buzzed in the background, as the evening team slowly organized their watch. Ian mumbled, "Nothing," before he punched more keys on his keyboard, eyes glued to the screen. Luke pushed away from the desk and stretched his legs in front of him.

"So why are we still here?"

The detective shot his partner an annoyed look then glared back at his computer.

"Why shoot this guy?"

Luke shrugged.

"A robbery gone sour? A pissed-off brother-in-law? I can find plenty of reasons, all of them perfectly pointless as long as we don't have an ID." Ian didn't budge. His friend plowed on, "We went through the whole database and the dental identification will take weeks at best."

"I know."

Ian finally distanced himself from the computer. He rubbed the five o'clock shadow on his chin.

"It's just… not making sense. This guy is dead, but no one is asking about him. He's not on the list of the missing, and no one rushed in to report a disappearance."

"I agree it's unusual, but not unheard of."

The blond linked his hands before him to make them crack.

"Is that your way of telling him to give it a rest until Monday?"

Luke grabbed his jacket on the back of his chair.

"Your words, not mine."

Ian logged out from the network.

"I gave to go and make sure Kermit didn't ravage my apartment anyway."

He answered the mute interrogation.

"My mother's cat. I'm housing it while she's in Europe to see my sister and the kids."

"Your mother called her cat Kermit?"

Luke entered the lobby, Ian on his heels.

"No, actually that was Ciaran's doing—"

The dark-haired man looked confused for a second before recognition hit him.

"That's your nephew, right?"

"Right." Ian grumbled under his breath. His brain circled around the image of the body on the tray in the morgue, again and again. Dead in a park, one shot in the back of the head, and no one had reported anything. No ID, no witness, no…

"Shit!"

"What?"

"Do we have pics of the scene?"

"Yeah, probably. Why?"

"I need to–"

"Braich? I have a delivery for Detective Braich!"

Looking over his shoulder to Ian, Luke nearly collided with a middle-aged man with a battered metallic pad in hand. His brand new parka was buttoned up to his neck. Perspiration pearled under his wool hat.

The next seconds crystallized, frozen in time like on a microfilm. Cold whipped in as two men entered the station. The pad reflected the late afternoon glow pouring in. The man dove one hand in his front pocket.

"Yes, he's right there."

Ian took the pen to sign the receipt then picked up the offered envelope. The ink on the sticker had faded. He ripped the envelope open. Luke said something about calling on Lauren.

The envelope contained a single sheet of paper folded in two. The outside door shook again. Ian lifted his eyes toward the noise. There was a hard clip about it, a chirp that reminded him of metal grinding against metal. He tackled the deliverer.

"Down!"

They hit the floor in a rain of plaster. The boom was deafening. Someone yelled. Ian reached for his gun, with nothing to aim at. His eyes burned. Breathing became a battle. People rushed around. Theirs screams shattered into whimpers. His ears pounded from the blast. Dust gave a ghostly shade to everything.

The deliveryman swayed, struggling to get on his knees. He blinked, as if the hands he held in front of him were not his. His palms were covered in blood and plaster. He rubbed them on his jeans, slowly at first, then frantically. The noise the friction of his sleeve made on his chest was nauseating.

Luke lay facedown, unmoving. Ian crawled on his forearms toward him. Shreds tore at his shirt. Shards of glass cut through. Blood pearled out of the gash. The metallic scent was everywhere around him. The tang invaded his lungs. He tasted nothing but blood. The volume increased until he heard nothing but yells. The motion accelerated to a dizzying speed.

"Officers down! Require immediate assistance! I repeat, need immediate assistance at the West station! Shit, we have wounded here!"

Ian pushed onto his knees. His vision channeled, blurred at the edge. He forced himself to stay still and breathe.

"Luke?"

His neck screamed in pain when he lifted his head. Ian struggled to stand. The walls reeled dangerously then caved. He realized it was him bending forward. Ian straightened up on shaky legs.

"Luke!"

He caught the banshee at the stairs, encaging her against his chest.

"Lauren, no, don't look."

She fought to break free. He tried to hold on tight, but his arms trembled. She shrieked, "Let me go!" Her voice pierced his eardrums. His muscles turned to jelly. He was ashamed to release her. He should be able to protect her from the hideous reality. His body shook as if he were standing on a wire, stretched high in the air during a storm.

The world spun out once more; the shouts around him muffled. Lauren was kneeling in the grime. She turned the body slowly. Luke's face was ashen. His elbow was turned at an unnatural angle. Ian swallowed. He didn't dare watch his friend's chest. It rose and fell, fragile as a plume in the breeze. Ian felt mesmerized by the sight. His heart threatened to explode. Someone took his arm, a shadow that stole the light around him.

"I'm fine. See to the others."

"Who did... you piss... off this time, Ian?" Luke heaved.

"Shush... Don't talk... Medic! Please, here! I need help!"

Luke's wheeze and Lauren's answer swirled in a cloud of white powder.

Sirens blared outside. It was hard to concentrate. The sheet of paper escaped his hand, its contents prophetic of the chaos around him.

*

The news of the attack was all over the local channels before midnight. While special units tried to keep journalists and other vultures at bay, Ian stayed out of the way as much as he could. His debriefing with the FBI and Homeland Security lasted less than twenty minutes, then they sent him home. He had little to say. He was leaving when a delivery guy came by asking for him. When he signed for the package, he had heard a noise, like a gun being cocked. Instinct had kicked in so he launched at the closest person while all hell broke loose. He didn't remember anything else.

Seated on his couch with the cat on his lap, he stared at the paper, not really seeing the words written on it.

'You've been warned.'

He should not have kept it from the FBI. He risked his badge if they found out. Ian realized it, yet he couldn't fathom one single reason he had gathered the paper and slipped it inside his jacket, leaving the old envelope empty into the feds' hands. Call it instinct once again. Or foolishness. The last couple of hours looked like some Hollywood action movie, with much more pain and a lot less entertainment.

Kermit yawned and stretched. Ian scratched his head, then dislodged the claws hooked in his shirt.

"Careful buddy, this hurts."

The cat shot him an unconcerned glare then moved to the other side of the couch where he sat and began grooming his paw, clearly uninterested in the whereabouts of the human beside him. Ian smiled despite the tiredness. Cats were cats: they cuddled if it suited them, and always on their terms.

He laid his head on the back of the sofa. The ceiling seemed to curve dangerously. Ian closed his eyes. Despite the buzz in his ears that refused to fade, the cuts and the bruises, he was lucky. Luke had a dislocated elbow, with multiple bone breaks in his left arm due to collapse of the memoria cabinet. One of the two police officers who had just entered the building when the front door exploded was dead from the deflagration. The other one was in critical condition.

The non-stop headlines on CNN had stopped talking about a terrorist attack and now referred to the mob. Explosives varied: bomb, mine, grenade launcher. Nothing made sense. Why hit a police station in a small city? It wasn't Al-Qaeda, or some craze.

Ian stared at the folded paper on the coffee table near the mug he hadn't touched.

'You've been warned.'

This was personal.

Chapter 8

Neve tried not to gasp when she stepped out of the
car. Large chunks of sandstone were missing, ugly scars
in the battered blackened façade. Steel sheets replaced the
front doors, which had been ripped out by the explosion.
Plastic tied with duct tape over the windows completed
the portrait.

Her heart sank. She pulled her zipper higher, more to
occupy her hands than anything else. Her eyes pricked,
and she knew it wasn't from cold. She was almost happy
Stefan had preferred to go with Lauren to the hospital to
see her brother. She wasn't sure she could have endured
his unstopping mouth now. Her own aggression seemed a
petty thing compared to the destruction in front of her.
She moved toward the building, then hesitated.

"We use the service door for now."

Neve spun, startled.

"Caleb!"

She took two steps toward the tall man. The flash of
surprise tainted with hope on his face stopped her at once.
Neve let her arms drop and settled for a smile.

"I'm glad you're all right."

The tall man shrugged.

"Yeah. Lucky to have been off duty, I guess. This way."

He pointed at the alley that led to the private parking lot and started toward it. Somehow it was easier when all she had to worry about was avoiding another invitation. Neve swallowed the growing lump in her throat and followed. Her gaze resolutely fixed on his back. The effort failed to help her ignore how much worse the walls looked at close range.

The back door opened on a corridor with lockers on one side, and what she supposed was a storage room on the other. Caleb strode toward another door that he pushed open for her. Heads snapped toward them, then shoulders relaxed when the few people gathered inside realized she wasn't a threat. Caleb walked through the war room without pausing, giving her no choice but to follow.

"You haven't told me why you've come."

Neve braced herself.

"Is Ian Braich here? I... I have to talk to him."

Caleb's physiognomy gloomed at once.

"His desk's over there. Good day."

The bearish man took off before she could even thank him. Left by herself, Neve padded toward the desk, unhooking her scarf. Stares ventured her way again, some curious, most of them distrustful. Maybe she should have called before coming? She touched her fingers to her collar absently.

"Neve."

The tired way he said her name yanked every nerve in her body so that her spin hurt.

"I've come to give my statement."

Ian gazed at her, blank faced. He looked worn out. She wanted to bang her head on the desk between them.

She wished she'd be able to tell how good it was to see him unharmed. Why couldn't she at least be civil to him?

"Right. The break-in."

It all came back with the scornful accent he put on his words. She pulled on the sides of her coat to arrange it on her shoulders.

"You know what, don't bother. I am dropping the charges. I didn't even want you to open a case in the first place. You have better things to do anyway," she motioned at the disaster around with her hand, "I'm sorry for all this, by the way."

The more she talked, the larger Ian's grin became. She felt like ripping it off his face with her nails, beaten or not.

"I wish I could indulge you, but you didn't press charges darling, your associate did."

"Don't call me 'darling'!"

Her voice rose to an unnatural octave. Neve took a deep breath to steady herself. The patient smile on her lips felt rigid.

"I thank you for your… concern. But I assure you it's unnecessary. I–"

"Braich! My office, now! And bring your guest with you!"

The captain's boom startled them both. Ian seethed between clenched teeth.

"You have a knack of putting me in trouble."

Just as riled, Neve replied on the same tone. "I'm pretty sure you don't need any help for that. If you had accepted to get off my–"

"Told you-."

"Braich! I don't have all day!"

*

"This is ludicrous. Please tell me you're kidding."

63

She chocked. Bourque furrowed his brows.

His face turned a nasty shade of purple. Ian braced himself for the explosion. The man wasn't used to being denied, and clearly he wasn't taking it well. He rolled his eyes at Neve who was glaring back.

"Do I look like I've got time to humor you, Miss Lass?"

"But–"

Ian chimed in.

"I am not going to babysit an amateur."

Neve bristled in indignation. He imagined for an instant her curls snapping like angry snakes. Her murderous glare certainly rivaled Medusa.

"I'm not–"

Bourque banged one fist on the table. The tepid coffee in his mug threatened to spill.

"Enough! I have two men dead, another incapacitated for at least five weeks. The FBI –not to mention the DHS– are on my back thanks to your '*lapse of memory,*' Braich. The mayor wants the vultures of the press off his. So I don't care if your professional agenda is full," he barked at Neve and Ian in turn. "I don't care if you don't like private and prefer working solo. You've got a license, and for what I hear, you attempted the Academy with some… success."

She paled as the captain snapped a file shut before him.

"Anyhow, so I requisition your services for the time being."

Neve sucked in air, clearly looking for an escape. Ian clamped his mouth closed so hard he nearly heard his jaw crack. She would try the patience of a saint. They had more chances to kill each other than achieve anything by *cooperating*. They hadn't even started and he already wanted to ditch her. Just as he opened his mouth to butt in, she swiveled impossibly vivid eyes on him.

"Ian, say something."

He'd never heard her pleading before. The room felt horribly small all a sudden. He ruffled his hair and pulled on his collar. Was it just him, or the thermostat was out?

Bourque groused, "Welcome to the VPD. Now get out of my office and get me results!"

The moment the door closed behind them, her mincing blew up to a full-scale blizzard.

"Why did you let him? I don't want to work with you!"

Ian grabbed her wrist so she would stop poking at his chest. People started to stare their way. He dragged her to an empty interrogation room and ushered her inside.

"Let me go right now or–"

"Or you what? Look, Lass, I'm stuck with you for the next couple of days or weeks, so it's time to set a few rules. First of all, stop taking me for your personal punching bag. Second–"

"You're such an oaf."

"Second, no insults during working hours."

Neve wriggled to free herself. He tugged lightly at her arms to force her to stay still.

"Listen to me, Neve."

"Release me first."

He obeyed, glancing at the one-way glass when she rubbed the tender skin above her hands.

"I'm as happy about this *arrangement* as you are. But I don't have a choice, and neither do you. So if you could stop being such a–"

He caught himself in time before the unsavory epithet that scorched the tip of his tongue enraged her further. Ian pinched the ridge of his nose.

"I don't have time for this…"

The chair legs rattled on the bare floor. He glowered as Neve sat down and crossed her legs. Her unctuous tone tempted him to wring her neck.

"Like you said, we don't have a choice. So–"

The chirp of her phone interrupted him. She nearly jumped on the excuse.

"Hi, Stefan… Yes, I'm at the station... No, we're not at each other's throat… Ah, Ah, you're hilarious… Oh good… Yes, I'll tell him… Sure… Yes… No!... Bye, Stefan."

Neve hung up and turned toward her reluctant new partner.

"Luke is doing fine, and he should be released in two days."

Ian sighed. His shoulders sagged a little; her expression softened. She offered a tentative smile.

"So, where do we start?"

He didn't answer immediately. Neve hesitated between trying again, and just abandoning him to his brooding. She stood.

"How about lunch?"

He smirked.

"Looking for neutral territory?"

She refrained from the need to grit her teeth. Why had he to make everything so difficult? Neve shrugged.

"I'm hungry."

"Me too."

This time, his smile was genuine and a bit sheepish. She debated letting it at that. Something nagged at the back of her mind.

"What did Captain Bourque mean when he talked about a 'lapse of memory'?"

"Don't ruin it, Lass," Ian groaned.

"You'll have to tell me eventually."

"You can't take peace when it's offered, can you?"

She sighed. The next weeks were going to be hell…
For the first time, and what she had a nasty feeling would
not be the last, Neve prayed to whoever looked after
female detectives to give her patience. Ian yanked the
door open but stepped out first. *Loads and loads of
patience…*

*

Their box was on the opposite wall, as far from the
crowd as possible. Not that the Bottom Stone was
overpopulated. At 11 a.m., it had just opened and, as their
host explained, people were less than keen to linger in the
neighborhood ever since the 'event.' Ian slipped into the
booth. His position gave him a good view of the bar. He
averted his eyes from the two portraits on the rear shelf,
wrapped in black. Neve noticed.

"I never had the chance to work with them…"

"I did."

She slapped her menu on the table at the forbidding
reply.

"Can't you at least make an effort to be civil? I'm
sorry they died, but not everything bad happening in your
life is my fault!"

"Are you sure?"

The question left her speechless. Ian pressed
forward.

"Don't you think it's a bit of a coincidence that my
station is bombed right after you're assaulted and I'm
commissioned to look into it?"

Neve hissed, "You commissioned yourself."

He brushed her comment aside.

"Random aggression happened in the street, for a
couple of bills or drugs. Stefan mentioned that you had
several intrusion attempts in the past month."

"It wasn't intrusions, just a windo–"

Neve hushed. Her forehead creased a little as she processed the possibility. She had never given it too much thought, because the fire escape was an old perilous thing several feet too short, but someone could have tried, someone looking for something in her office… She'd been a casualty, at the wrong place at the wrong moment. When her eyes widened slightly, Ian interrupted her rumination.

"What have you been working on?"

Flushing and just a little riled, she grumbled under her breath, "The P in PI means Private you know."

Ian leaned forward, invading her personal space. Neve jerked back in her seat. He smirked.

"You can tell me, or I can seize your computer and ask Caleb to check."

"As if your team hadn't ravaged the place already."

"It wasn't us. Whoever knocked you out did quite a job searching the desks and the file cabinets, but they didn't touch the computer. What were they looking for?"

"How should I know? I don't have anything!" She deflated within the next breath. "I don't understand… I'm not some new version of Sam Spade! I investigate suspicious claims for insurance companies. I look for missing people, that kind of thing… I have authenticity certificates, expert reports, pictures, nothing that is worth all that…"

Ian kept quiet. He couldn't say he cared for the sparkles that wet her stare.

Chapter 9

Fragrant whiffs swirling from the parsnip-pear potage teased his nostrils to remind him he hadn't had breakfast. The young man grabbed his spoon at once to attack the croutons, wolfing them down two at a time. Neve crooked an eyebrow.

"I don't like them spongy."

She grinned at the giveaway then attacked her own meal with gusto. Ian swallowed another spoonful. The pub was filling up despite the previous assertion of slow business. At the moment, most of the patrons stayed close to the bar. But soon, quiet conversation would be impossible.

"Tell me more about your current case."

Neve glanced up irresolute for a few seconds before she complied.

"Did you hear about the Hills Fire? The owner had contracted insurance for several porcelains, including an eighteenth blue faience, typical of the Dutch East India Company. It was insured for about half a million, so T-AIG wants to make sure it really burned."

Ian whistled through his teeth.

"Was the fire accidental?"

"That's what the fire department concluded, despite the very high temperature. Apparently the fire reached more than 2000 degrees, due to the wooden shelves–" Neve trailed off, suddenly conscious of the heavy stare focused on her. She gave an apologetic smile.

"Lauren sent me a detailed report about the fragments we collected. I skirted through it, but I need to read it again. I'm not sure I gathered all the technicalities."

He shot her a pointed look.

"Right. Lauren's good with… technicalities. Did you work for that company before? What do you know of the owner?"

"Yes, and nothing much. The man built his own import/export business. Died two years ago. His widow made the claim." Neve shrugged. "She's more concerned about the money than the art loss or the house. I don't see why she would interfere with the investigation."

The insurance company was one of the most famous in the U.S. for fine art protection. They didn't build their business by cheating on contracts. The more she tried to fit the pieces together, the less the whole image made sense. Apparently, Ian reached the same conclusion.

"Is that your only open case?"

"Yes. I was also asked to look into a music libretto parentage, but I had to put it on hold until I reported my conclusion on this one."

"Who hired you?"

"Some obscure self-published Canadian author. I don't remember the name, it sounded French."

The waiter bringing their brie sandwiches cut short any questions Ian might set his doubts about the request. He waited until the man moved away with their empty bowls to fire into another direction. "The intrusion began last month. What were you at the time?"

Neve frowned in concentration.

"I'm not sure. We were very busy last fall, so when things quieted in December, we used the spare time to do some paperwork, close the financial year with the accountant, that kind of thing. We gave some time to the community, and then it was Christmas."

Ian didn't answer. He bit into his sandwich. The French cheese enrobed turkey in warmth. The cook had added bananas pickles for spice and fresh slices of green apples for sweet. The dressing on his side salad was olive oil based, and just as perfect.

Neve sampled her own, her eyes fluttering closed when the same explosion of savors teased her tongue.

"Hum…"

Ian laughed. She flushed a deep pink. He washed his bite with water and teased, "So we do agree on some things after all…"

She pouted, though pleasure sparkled in her gaze.

"You have told me about your part of the bargain, helping me to find who wants to mess up my practice. What's mine?"

Ian took another mouthful. Neve squinted at him. He chewed on, unconcerned by the piercing gaze. Their little contest lasted for half a minute before her eyes suddenly cleared.

"It's about the explosion… You know something… Bourque said…" Neve covered her mouth with one hand "Oh my God, you concealed evidence from the FBI!"

He glowered.

"Wrong. The feds have everything I laid my hands onto."

Ian made a show of picking up his glass so the ice cubes tilted. She narrowed her eyes. He wasn't telling her the whole truth, and he knew she knew. Neve waited, watching his every move. He held the eye contest without a blink. She retained a grunt. He needed her help, but didn't want it. Her patience thinned. *Damned infuriating misogynist who-*

"A man was found dead in the park last week. Gunshot, but not on site. No blood. We searched all databases. He doesn't exist. I need to find who he is, and who put him there. Bodies don't appear out of nowhere. Someone must have seen something."

Dumbfound, she opened her mouth to speak. Ian leaned forward.

"Neve," something in his tone killed the argument before she voiced it out loud, "I'm only working this case in addition to yours, and someone bombed a police station to keep me out of it."

Her eyes popped wide.

"You think the two are linked?"

"Homeless people don't talk to cops, but they will with someone they trust. You have the connections. Ask around. Someone must know that guy, or has seen something. This *is* important. Because either I've been warned about that murder, or it was about you."

They finished their meal in silence. Neve spooned her coffee, mulling the elements he had given her. A part of her still rebelled at the idea of pairing up with Ian. Another longed to prove to him she was as good a detective as he was. She wasn't sure which thought disturbed her the most.

"So what do we do now?"

Ian drained his cup and stood.

"*We* do nothing. I'm going back to work, and you to your cleaning."

Neve gaped. Did he just…

"I beg your pardon?"

"Trust me, sweetheart, I would love to hear you beg, but I really have to get going."

"You're unbelievable!"

That was the gentler adjective she could use without swearing. Ian sneered, not even bothering to look at her in the eye as he dropped a couple of bills on the table.

"I thought we were–"

He squeezed her arm. Neve jolted away to no avail. His grab was strong enough to bruise. His undertone froze the curse on the tip of her tongue when Ian growled.

"The guy screening the room on your right is with the FBI. I don't want him to get in our way just yet."

"I…"

Her eyes shone suspiciously. Neve pulled away and screeched.

"I'm so fed up with you!"

Then she slapped him as hard as she could. Angry bees swarmed in his eardrums. He drew a deep breath to cover the shock. Air went down the wrong pipe and he gagged. Neve whacked his back lightly. The small pat and gentle circles only seemed to bring out a new fit. He wanted to bark to shove her off. Indignation reduced to a lamentable meow. Air filled his lungs with vicious hisses; tears welled in his eyes.

Before he could even manage to drag in air to straighten up, his personal space crowded with curves and silken hair.

"Oh, Ian…"

Neve locked her arms around his neck, pulling his head down to hers. His ego rebelled while male instinct kicked hard to pick up the offering. What did she think she was doing? The hellcat scratched his face and now… She stood on her tiptoes to murmur.

"Just help with the show, all right?"

Show. Ah yes...

Neve felt the hand on her hip tighten its grip. She tried not to blush. His strong body was warm against hers, the resilient coughs forcing them into a strange brushing dance. Firm lips found hers and she lost her breath in a humph. Ian kept the kiss chaste, moving his mouth over hers gently, almost tenderly. Her toes curled. She had to resist the need to angle her head backward to help his caress. She hadn't really expected that one touch would be enough to sweep her off her feet.

Her top hiked up as Ian enfolded her into his arms. The chill yielded to him as well. The hard grip in the small of her back was more than pleasant. Someone catcalled in the background, far, far away. Not drowning into the kiss grew harder by the second. Her world swirled madly around her, her feet leaving the ground, and then...

Air sneaked into her lungs, almost unwelcome. Ian released her too fast for her taste, and yet gently enough so that she didn't lose her footing. Her knees felt like rubber. She lifted one hand up as if to steady herself, trembling not to fist his shirt for more. Ian smirked, and the pleasant warmth dissolved.

He wet his lips. She had just given them the escape route he was asking for. The whole exchange looked like lovers bickering. If the agent asked around, everybody who knew them would tell him they fight like cats and dogs more often than not, dismissing it as another tantrum in a rocky love story. He had no reason to be annoyed, let alone embarrassed.

The idea had crossed his mind once or twice in the past anyway, so why not? Neve was drop-dead gorgeous, intelligent, spirited...

"So are you coming?"

And absolutely infuriating. The stunning woman was standing between him and the door, arms crossed over her chest and her foot building up a rhythm on the floor. Ian thought briefly to punch the barman's laughing face.

74

A mop of gray hair in the back wobbled suspiciously too. FBI was smirking.

Her fingers trailed fire up his forearm until they branded his elbow, guiding him out of the bar. Ian blinked, a part of him suspicious and the other too alert of the way her long ponytail danced in rhythm with her hips.

"Neve!"

She finally consented to stop and faced him. He rustled his hair, ill at ease. She didn't look self-assured herself.

"Please don't. I brought you out of it, but just… Don't."

Ian retreated a safe three feet away. His neck burned from the need to glimpse inside to see if FBI was still looking. Neve read his mind and shook her head. He released a long sigh, then nodded.

That was what she liked best about him. When he wanted to, he kept up with her without endless explanations. He outstripped her in the shooting sarcasm range. He was stronger, though she was quicker on her feet. And now, she could add mind-blowing kisser to his talents' list. Not that it mattered; much. She frowned to hide her smile.

"Next time, I would appreciate a little warning."

"As do I."

Her grin crystalized on her lips. She glared, her back stiffened. Ian winked, clearly proud of his joke. The manhandling and prating she liked definitely less.

"It was your ide—"

"Just admit it, Neve, you wanted to kiss me…"

She stopped herself just in time before she asked if he had ever heard about sexual harassment. One look confirmed the agent from Homeland Security had not followed them. She jumped out of reach.

"I can walk by myself, thank you."

He chuckled, but accepted the rebuff.

The cold made the perfect excuse to walk briskly. Neve brushed off the lost snowflakes that started to cling to her parka. This association was a bad idea… Not that she had been offered much of a choice. *Bad, bad idea…*

RECKLESS ILLUSIONS

Chapter 10

"Doc said I was lucky," Luke said and groaned as Lauren helped him up in his bed. "A couple of inches to the left, and the femoral vein would have been crushed."

Ian winced. Luck was a question of perspective. His partner had had his knee partly reconstructed, and they had put a steel bar in his right thigh. He would probably need a cane for the rest of his life. And even if he didn't, he would be stuck behind a desk.

"Hey, stop with the self-flogging and gloomy face, will you? Tell me what's happening. What do we know?"

Lauren shot him a glare from the other side of the bed. Ian ignored the warning. Luke needed to be kept in the loop as much as he needed to discuss this with his partner; his real partner.

"Not much. The FBI is leading the investigation."

"Bourque probably loved that."

The brunette patted the pillows a tad harder. Luke glanced up at his sister. This time, Ian took the hint.

"All right, I'll call you in a few days, okay?"

"Sure. I'll just rest, and enjoyed the nurses' attentions. They can't have worse bedside manners than my sister anyway."

Lauren rolled her eyes. She shrugged at Stefan, as if saying '*See what I have to endure*', but relief brightened her stare. Ian nodded with a grin. He got to his feet.

"You'll do that."

They lingered in the room a few more minutes. Finally, the doctor chased them away to examine his patient in peace. Stefan used the distraction to approach Ian.

"Did you see Neve?"

Ian dismissed the question, his attention suddenly attracted by a familiar silhouette coming toward them.

"Yes, she's going to help."

What was that guy doing here? Were the feds following him?

"Help?"

Lauren zeroed suspicious eyes on Ian. Stefan looked just as baffled. The blond man hissed under his breath.

"Not now, Lauren.

"Mr. Beneto?"

Ian frowned. The man wasn't addressing him obviously, but then- His jaw half-slackened when he saw Stefan jerk upright, pale as a sheet.

"It's Benedict. My name is Stefan Benedict."

The man in black in front of him welcomed the rebuff with a shark smile, all teeth, and no warmth whatsoever.

"Funny. My notes here say Stefano Beneto. Anyhow, can I have a word with you?"

Ian stared at the culprit air on Neve's assistant's face while the name sank in. Bells rang in alarm in his ears, loud enough for him to miss Stefan's muttered agreement before the two men stepped aside. The Benetos had served as *Caporegimi* and soldiers in the New York Mafia, still active despite the RICO Act. They had handled most of the dirty business in gambling and drugs, until another family had accused them of tying roots with the Limone in Boston. The avalanche of information that crashed down on him in the last few days was too much to absorb at once.

Lauren tugged at his arm.

"Ian, what's happening? Why is he–"

"I don't know. Listen."

He escaped the grip to approach Stefan and asked, "Does Neve know?"

It came out wrong. It wasn't what he wanted to ask. FBI glowered.

"Detective Braich, I understand that you have a personal interest in this investigation, but I don't appreciate your interference. I thought your captain made that clear."

Ian held the angry stare without a blink.

"He did. Stefan?"

"You don't have to answer the police question, Mr. Beneto, this is strictly federal business."

The idea to punch both men in the face crossed his mind. Ian sucked in air in an attempt to rein his temper. He croaked, "I'll talk to you later."

He wasn't precise about to whom the comment was addressed before he turned and walked away. Stefan's guilty look escorted him all the way to his car.

*

Contrary to what she told Ian, Neve didn't go straight back to her office. She'd had a look yesterday. What the thief had not overturned or ripped open, the police had covered in print powder. She hadn't even realized she stored so many documents until she saw all those papers carpeting the wood floor. She would have to,; eventually, if she couldn't coerce Stefan into cleaning the mess for her. After that strange dinner, and even stranger exit, she couldn't fathom the strength to face the chaos yet again. What she needed was air.

Turning left at the end of the street, she chose to head toward the park and Ian's mysterious John Doe. Neve gazed at the gray and white patchwork in front of her, hands curled around the wheel. She doubted she could gather any intel' the police hadn't already. Even though Ian was sure his elusive witnesses would open up to someone who wasn't wearing a badge, things were rarely that simple.

The chances that someone indeed saw something were slim. The cold wave had chased even the hard-corers of the streets to shelters. If anyone had stayed behind, they would have cuddled under as many layers of rags and newspaper as possible and stay hidden in a corner as far away from open space as possible.

In winter, the road circling the park was opened to traffic. Neve entered it from the south. She drove around at a snail's pace, looking for an opening in the snow drifts to park. The white field reflected the pale afternoon shine to make her eyes water. The L shape of the Art Gallery was clearly visible through the bare trees, flanking the park on its north and west sides. The Arcades on her right housed two restaurants and the usual souvenir shops. Those as well as the glacier were closed for the season.

She spotted the yellow tape that marked the crime scene location. The bench was only a yard or two from one of the diagonal paths that crisscrossed the park. A car could have access it without too much trouble.

Neve let the tires bite slightly in the snow and stopped the car. Each building was several hundred yards from the spot. She stepped out and shaded her eyes to rake over the snowfield to convince herself of what she already knew. No one sheltered in the back alleys near the Gallery or the Arcades could have seen anything useful at this distance, assuming that someone was there in the first place. It was just ridiculous, and a waste of time.

She shook her head and opened her door. As if on cue, her phone chirped. She fumbled with the zipper of her breast pocket, cursing the cold and her wool gloves. By the time she managed to extract the phone, a text message appeared on the screen.

'We need to talk.'

Her eyes shot daggers at the screen. If they were to work together, he'd have to learn about manners. The ringer belled again before she could punch an answer to the clip words.

"You know, Ian, you could start with hel–"

Neve gagged. The voice menacing her wasn't Ian's.

'...or you will regret it.'

The hair on her nape bristled.

"Who are you? What do you want?"

The hang-up silence drilled in her ears. Neve darted her eyes around. The park was deserted. She pounced more than climbed into her seat, banging the door behind her, heart thumping. Her fingers fumbled with the keys on the ignition.

*

'My office, thirty minutes.'

Ian scowled. Where the hell was she? Hadn't he told her to go to her office? He slapped his hands together to warm them. He had to be nuts, freezing his butt on a sidewalk so she could explain why she omitted mentioning her assistant was a member of the mob. The attack made so much sense now...

"What are you doing?" a slightly familiar voice said.

He spanned his head around, very annoyed not to have heard the old man coming up behind him.

"Mr. Whale."

The caretaker pointed his chin forward.

"Looking for clues?"

Ian glared toward the side alley. The asphalt had been wiped clean earlier in the day, the fresh snow now piled along the building. If there had been any, the wind and shoveling had erased footprints or other marks. He snorted, and looked up to the emergency staircase. The metallic frame was folded. Despite his 6 feet 2 inches, he had to stand on tiptoe to grab it. His gloved hand slipped on the metal, but took hold of the frozen bar. The pin whined horribly as he pulled it down. Small chips of ice peppered his face.

"I don't think anyone used that ladder," his companion commented.

Ian tested his weight on the first step, not bothering with an answer.

"I don't recommend you climb up. Those things are decrepit. You could get hurt."

He wasn't in the mood for another amateur playing detective.

"Then you should stand back while I'm doing my job."

Ian saw the old caretaker shrug from the corner of his eye. The metal groaned into a screech as he hauled himself higher. The wind shook the precarious staircase so he trudged up. Maybe the climb wasn't such a good idea after all. No one had been up this way in years. The window really needed repairs, and the attack on Neve was Stefan's fault.

Ice chips dropped like rain on his head. The chill sluiced under his collar. Ian ducked his head between his shoulders.

"Ian!"

He lifted his eyes to find Neve looking down on him from the infamous window.

"Stop shouting, you're going to bring the whole thing down on my head. I'm coming up."

"The opening is too high, you–"

He climbed the last steps two by two until he reached the window. His shoulders towered above the frame by inches. Ian steadied his grip on the rail and hauled himself up with a groan. Neve had backed into the room, but she moved forward again to help him inside. He huffed, "Your burglar didn't come this way."

She raised an eyebrow as he shook his parka.

"I could have told you that…"

"You also could have told me about your association with the local mob."

Neve gaped.

"What?"

"Stefan's real name is Stefano Beneto. Ring any bells?"

"Yes, I know, but–"

Ian clamped the window shut.

"But what? It wasn't worth mentioning? You were assaulted inside your own office, Neve! And right after that someone bombed the police station!"

"And you're blaming Stefan for it?" Her voice shrilled with disbelief and anger. Her tawny eyes blazed.

"Get out."

Neve turned her back to him, moving around the room to gather papers on the floor and slammed them on her desk. He waited. The hostile silence grew, heavier by the minute. Out of patience, Ian called out.

"Neve."

"I don't have to suffer your contempt or your accusations. Get. Out," she hammered with one finger pointing at the door and her back to him, peering at some papers on the desk. He stood his ground.

"I will as soon as you'll give me the full story."

84

"I'm dropping the charges. So this place is no longer a crime scene, and you're trespassing."

"Again, this is not your call to make."

She finally turned. He held the burning stare that tried to drill him into the ground. If looks could kill... A phone rang. Neve paled, her hand jerking away from her pocket as if she got burned. Her gaze flickered toward the window behind him. Ian frowned.

"What is it?"

"I–"

He took the phone from her hand and watched the screen. The number started with the mandatory eight-something, as all toll free numbers.

"Probably your client."

"Yes, maybe..."

Yet she made no gesture to take the phone back. She looked scared. Something new, and not at all welcomed. Ian put the phone on her desk then moved to the couch without another word. Neve seemed to hesitate. Taking a deep breath, she joined him. He noticed she squeezed her hands between her knees. It took another minute before she started talking.

*

Stefan had shown up after she posted an opening for an assistant, three years ago. He was new to town with no experience whatsoever. During his interview, he had managed to knock off his cup of coffee, ruining a report she'd been working on for two days. By the time he finished apologizing, her decision was made. Stefan was friendly, he talked too much and was a walking disaster, but she was buried under work, he was the only candidate, but his good humor was contagious, and yes, she liked him.

However, before he agreed to take the job, Stefan had given away the big secret. His cousin had cut a deal with the FBI, in exchange for safe conduct for the rest of the family. Stefan, his aunt and his mother had been given new identities, and relocated.

Neve stared at her hands, palms clasped together. This way, they didn't tremble so much.

"I can't believe Stefan has anything to do with all this…"

"And I don't believe in coincidences."

Ian's tone had lost its edge, though it remained strong as steel. Neve lifted her gaze to the holster under his arm then his face.

"But why?"

"The answer lies somewhere in the cases you worked on."

A sharp rap on the door interrupted them. Neve straightened up.

"Come in."

Terence's head appeared as the caretaker nudged the door ajar.

"Miss Neve; I just wanted to let you know I called in a carpenter to look at this window."

"Thank you."

Ian used the diversion to stand.

"I have to go back to the station. Remind Stefan that I need his statement too when you see him."

Neve shot him a puzzled look. If he wanted to talk to Stefan about his past why didn't he say so instead of…

The old man cleared his throat so she swallowed back her comment and nodded.

"I will. Thanks for… the update. I hope you'll find a lead soon."

"I'll see myself out. Give me a call if anything else comes up."

While his back disappeared in the corridor, Neve realized she hadn't told him about her deductions on the park murder, or about the other call. She felt like a piece on a chessboard at the beginning of a new game, unaware of the players' strategy, and with no idea which figure she was, a pawn, a fool or the queen.

Chapter 11

The man took the time to turn down his CD player before picking up the phone.

'*You promised she would not get hurt.*'

"And *you* promised to recover the information a long while ago. Our patience is not infinite."

'*And look at the results! Braich is going to put his nose everywhere now.*'

"Ian's not half of the man his father was. Leave Braich to us."

'*You're underestimating him; he's tenacious and Neve will want to prove herself to him, she always does.*'

"I strongly suggest you concentrate on your own mission. I want information in the next twenty-four hours. If not, someone could learn about your alter-ego…"

'*But–*'

The man put the receiver back on its cradle. He stood, and walked to observe the purple sky darkening. Forecast promised another cold day. He would have preferred snow. The biting cold seemed to always find a way to gnaw at his bones. When this was settled once and for all, he'd take a ticket for a long trip, and go back to Europe. He smirked at his reflection.

How did they say? *See Naples and die.*

*

Ian headed home. He just couldn't go and sit at his desk just now. He tried the radio, and shut it off within the same movement. Even the ticking noise of the flashers rattled his nerves. He kept his eyes on the road, not really seeing the gray-white snake in front of him. Information rattled in his head like pieces of an unfinished puzzle. Every time they collided, he hoped for the biggest picture to appear, to no avail.

Could Stefan really be the culprit? It didn't make sense to accuse Stefan Benedict, who had a complete access to whatever he wanted in the office and plenty of occasions to gather it discreetly. But what of Stefano Beneto? Did getting a new name and a new life erase his name from the plate completely? An old acquaintance could have found him. Then why break into the PI's office, instead of coming at Stefan in the street, in a coffee shop or else? That was the safest way to attract attention. The Vallon wasn't Boston, or New York. Organized Crime wasn't as powerful, and it only held a quarter of the power they had held in the past. The pieces refused to fit together and swirled and whirled.

He turned left and then right, not really paying attention to the direction he was going and unsure why he needed the constant motion forward so badly. The last two days felt like a lifetime. Ian took the next street on his right again. The last time he felt that tired was... He couldn't pinpoint when it was. After that three days' vigil as a rookie maybe? That was before he was paired up with Luke. Guilt waltzed in. He really should have gone back to the station, at least to give another shot at the autopsy report, or to take his turn at the 24-hour hot line.

There were too many thoughts waving in his head. Too many questions, and not one hint of an answer.

The red lights on the car before him startled him. Ian jumped on the breaks. The car skidded slightly then stopped. Heart pounding, he finally checked his surroundings, and took in the heavy iron gates at the entrance of St. Georges Cemetery.

The nine-year-old boy padded toward the stairs. He was supposed to do math. His teacher had added another four exercises to his plate because he had failed last week's test by far. He didn't care. He bet police officers didn't need long division. His dad never talked about doing math, did he?

He would labor his way through it eventually, at least before his mom checked. At the moment, she was clapping her hands together lightly to clean the last whiff of flour from them before she answered the door. They were having homemade pie for dessert.

Ian fidgeted with the sleeves of his Batman sweatshirt. It was early for his father to be home. And his dad never rang the bell, he had a key. Ian had one too, now. Last year, he'd been considered old enough and was offered the key to the house. His tiny chest puffed with pride at the memory. Maybe he should make an effort, and finish those divisions.

His father had promised to take him skating after work, if his homework was done. He only had two more to go. Not that he was overconfident, with the last one it took him more than half an hour to solve. Having 123 times 7 in 168 felt wrong somehow. He balanced on his heels back and forth, peeking at his bedroom and the hall in turn. Curiosity won. He peered down again, and got a peek of navy blue between his mother's raised arm and the door.

"Dad?"

His mom half-turned and the boy froze. Her face was white, and twisted. She clamped one hand to her mouth but the sound that escaped was so raw he tumbled backward.

"Mommy?"

"Ian, come with me."

"Ann', why does Mom–"

"Come."

His big sister took his hand and tugged him away from the stairs. She was eleven, but she didn't sass over it. Ian squirmed under the bone-crushing grip.

"You're hurting me."

"I... I'm sorry."

She apologized, but she kept grasping nonetheless. Her face looked all funny, with her big blue eyes shining. Ian felt his stomach squeeze. He clutched her hand as hard as she was.

"Annie, what's happening? Where's Dad?"

Ian swallowed the lump in his throat. Twenty-three years later, everything else had blurred, like an old movie, but that particular memory.

Much later, he had learned the bomb was in the trunk. The witness his father was bringing to court was in the back seat and had been killed instantly; his father? Not so lucky. The shockwave had snapped his spine in two. The loss of blood had damaged his brain. It had taken three more years for him to die. Three years of visits to the hospital, of trying to connect the image of the waxen rag doll in the bed with the strong man who used to play ball and skate with him. Three years of hell, and twenty more to remember it.

The young man pressed his hands deeper in his pockets, taking comfort from the hard mass of his Glock against his ribs. Breathing was like dragging ice into his lungs. Ian shrugged, and walked back to his car.

*

Installed on the couch in her office with her feet on the edge of the coffee table, Neve skimmed over the same page for the fourth time. She read the words, understood most of them, but the meaning behind Lauren's precise writing eluded her. Neve turned another page, ogled at the colorful graph; each peak was labeled with tiny letters that referred to the chemical they represented. Lauren had circled the largest one in red with a note: 'Large amount of copper present'.

She looked at her notes on the laptop beside her: 'presence of tin oxide'; 'typical cooked clay signature'; 'dating impossible due to state of samples'. Her own research on Delftware characteristics claimed that she had enough to wrap up her own report, and confirmed to her client that the insured plate was indeed in the warehouse and now lost. She'd got that on her first reading. But it didn't explain...

Neve leaned back on the couch, skirting to the end of the report. The 3D model the forensic tech had built up showed a truncate trumpet bell of some sort. There weren't enough pieces to complete the form, but the software had extrapolated a top merely larger than the base. Lauren hypothesized it was antique bronze. If so, why the owner hadn't insured it as well? Not that it mattered. Lauren's doubts about the plate's support were not part of her mandate. She was crossing the line, as usual... Neve sighed, rolling her neck to ease its ache.

It was nearly 6 p.m. The opened curtains framed a dark, empty sky. The late afternoon clouds had drifted away to bare the moon. The pale gibbousness promised another artic cold day. She pulled on her sleeves to bury her fingers in the wool folds. Suddenly she missed the sun and the suffocating days of summer in New England, when humidity and heat thickened the air until breathing felt like sucking in warm water. Neve looked away from the window to study her office.

She still had to sort the papers she had piled on the desk. Her elbow propped up on the back seat, she rubbed the bridge of her nose. Terence's announcement about a carpenter coming gave a great excuse not to sweep the room up. But she would have to clear the hazardous pile near the phone. She didn't want to think about the phone. It rang and rang, but every time she picked up the receiver, she only heard a disconnecting click. Looking at the phone increased the pressure between her brows. In a way, the piercing beep was worse than the threats.

"Hi!" The laptop catapulted up, then bounced on the cushion.

"Stefan!"

"I was worried; you weren't at the apartment and your phone is off…"

Neve grasped her computer tighter to steady her fingers. Stefan flushed.

"Sorry. I thought you had heard me in the corridor. Terence said–"

"Yes… Yes I know. God, you scared me…"

Neve removed the report just in time as her friend slumped on the couch beside her. Stefan shrugged with an apologetic smile.

"Sorry… So, what's up?"

She pondered over the multiple ways she could answer the question. The words streamed out before she could finish the list.

"I told Ian."

"Good. He was here when the feds came over anyway."

"Good? Stefan, he thinks I was attacked because of you!"

"Maybe he's right."

Neve shifted to take a better look at her friend. He focused on the screen of the laptop instead, picking up the report in his free hand. He hadn't even taken his scarf off.

"Stefan, what is it? What did the FBI want?"

"They want me to testify in court against the Underboss."

Neve jerked upright on the couch.

"You? But you know nothing!"

"I know enough."

"But they have your cousin for that. You said–"

Stefan pulled at one extremity of his scarf to whip it off. When it fell off, he leaned forward, his elbows on his knees, head up to meet her stare.

"Neve, my cousin disappeared from his safe house. No one has seen him since January 24th. Either he took off, or he's dead. Whatever the case, if they don't bring a witness to court it will be a hard blow. Not to mention the guy will be free."

For the first time since he passed her threshold, Neve saw worry in the blue eyes fixed on her. Sadness filled them, a concern way behind the usually merry man's age. She worried her bottom lip, torn between a need to escape and the urge to comfort and be comforted.

"When are you leaving?"

Stefan's gaze dropped.

"Tomorrow or the day after that. They need time to arrange a new safe house. Why did you shut the phone off? If you need me–"

Neve shook her head and stood. She grabbed her parka from its hook.

"I just wanted to work in peace. Don't worry about it. Let's go home."

"Am I off the cooking?"

She put the alarm on, and let Stefan escort her out of the room.

"Maybe; but just this time."

*

Ian stepped inside his apartment to find Kermit waiting behind the door. That was more than the cat had granted him in the past three weeks. Ian picked up the cat.

"Hey, you."

The feline rubbed his head against his shoulder, purring, then pedaled to get free. Ian released him to take off his jacket. The answering machine blinked on the kitchen counter top. He pressed the listen button, and get at once why the cat was so worked up.

'Ian? It's Mom... We heard... Oh my God, are you hurt? They said two people are dead, and another is in the hospital. Please call me as soon as you get this. I can be home tomorrow if you need me. Please call me; I love you.'

Kermit meowed. The anguish in his mother's voice tugged hard. Ian grabbed the phone.

Chapter 12

Neve stared at the man seated in front of her and wondered once more how they were going to manage and work together. This time, it had taken a grand total of five minutes before they started exchanging sugar-coated barbs. Ian questioned her deductions; she accused him of sending her on a wild goose chase. He pushed, she balked, and if she didn't shut her mouth right this minute, she was going to remark about harassment and sexism. Or tear his throat apart with her teeth. Or both. The sardonic curve of his mouth was just too much.

"Look, you asked me to look into it. Now if you don't like the results–"

Ian lost his smirk.

"Why don't you tell me why you're trying so hard to pick a fight?"

"I'm not–"

She clammed up once more. Ian leaned forward so that she couldn't escape his piercing gaze.

"There's something you're not telling me, and if we want this association to work, you have to trust me."

"Says the pot to the kettle," Neve seethed under her breath. Ian's lips twitched; had she been less furious, she would have sworn the flicker in his blue-gray eyes contained a solid dose of amusement as well.

"Touché. So, what's the matter with you?"

She bit back a ferocious urge to send him to hell. He would just come back from it with that same infuriating look on his face.

Neve drew out a breath. The annoyance settled, baring the doubts and the worries that kept her awake half the night. She nibbled at her lip, looking for the simplest way to tell him about Stefan, and the phone calls. Ian scanned her face for a moment longer. He finally looked away to fish a file from the documents littered on his desk and pushed it toward her.

"I'll start, then. I agree about the park. We don't have a witness because there 'asn't one. It was a long shot."

He locked hands behind his head. Neve opened the folder gingerly. The photographs were crude shots of the corpse. Neve scanned them over as quickly as she could, then squinted at the autopsy report clipped on the left side. Ian summarized the conclusions for her.

"One shot, from behind in the back of the head. The bullet's caliber is .22. The medical examiner said the victim wasn't restrained at the time of death but possibly before; there are no post mortem wounds, but traces of intense hypothermia."

"That's not really a surprise, the poor man was left outside nearly naked…"

Ian nodded in agreement.

"They tried to cover the murder up."

She grabbed a pen to play with, the report still on her lap. He watched the stick swirled back and forth around her thumb. The pen moved one way, then the other, left, right, left and right again, until she missed her shot and it flew on the floor. Neve secured the folder with one hand before she bent over to grab her toy, calling from under,

"Why kill this guy? I mean, what's the motive? Obviously it was premeditated, so–"

Neve straightened up, her cheeks flushed from the dive. Ian's stare had hardened again, though this time the scowl assaulted someone behind her. She half-turned in her chair to catch sight of a dark jacket, and an open badge.

"Special Agent Martin, FBI."

Ian snorted.

"I thought you federal lot always came as a pair; where's Scully?"

Neve glowered at the blond detective in front of her while patting the loose curls that had escaped from her braid. Ian didn't pick up the cue and said, "So, what can I do for you?"

The unctuous tone dripped with sarcasm. Her already-pink cheeks flamed. She muttered 'Watch your mouth' under her breath while unfolding her legs to stand. Her ankle hit the sharp edge of the table feet. She yelped.

The FBI agent broke his staring contest with Ian to look down at her.

"Anything wrong, Miss Lass?"

"No, yes, I'm fine… Just a false move. Humph…"

Her grimace and groan told otherwise. Ian pushed to his feet, using his hands on the desk as leverage. The motion made the holster on his side bulge.

"And, how, exactly, do you know her name?"

Martin stored his badge back inside his jacket.

"Actually, Detective, I know a lot of things." Neve stopped rubbing her sore knee to glance up. This time Ian held his tongue. "You've been so welcoming I feel I can only repay the kindness by sharing some of them. Shall we?"

The FBI agent pointed toward the corridor leading to the back. Neve imitated him and pushed onto her feet.

She grimaced when she unfolded her right leg. The detective caught her elbow.

"I'd rather you stay here."

"I'd like to hear what he has to say, actually."

Ian's nostrils flared. She offered a brilliant smile despite the pain, and limped after Martin.

*

The bitter tang floating around the morgue assaulted his nose as soon as he entered. Ian swallowed. The room reeked of bleach, and whatever chemical they used to clean the place. The door clenched back into place with a disagreeable click.

The young man cast a glance to his right. Martin was already examining the bottles and instruments around. Neve was standing in a corner, as far from the fridge door as possible, her back straight as an 'I'. Her cheeks had paled considerably, her luscious lips sealed tight as if she, too, tried to inhale as little air as possible. When she lifted dilated eyes to his face, he nodded in encouragement. Her gaze reminded him of a doe caught in a truck's headlights. He couldn't fathom why Martin had brought them here.

Ian cleared his throat.

The man in black put the pad down on a nearby box. The scalpels rattled. Without a word, he counted three doors in the middle row and pulled. The tray rolled out. It stopped with a clang that buried Neve's gasp. The shiny tray was empty.

Ian marched on the FBI investigator. He snarled, "I don't believe the melodrama was necessary."

"And I don't believe you realize the mess your reckless intervention has created."

Caught off guard, Ian shut up. Martin leaned forward and wrenched the file from Neve's loose hands. The photographs spilled on the stainless tray.

"This... is how more than twenty years of effort are reduced to dust."

"Agent Martin, I'm sorry to hear that but how–"

Ian interrupted her question.

"I searched every possible database, why didn't I get at least a warning about him being involved in special ops?"

"Ian..." Neve's fingers sunk in his forearm. Her eyes vibrated with recognition. She detached her gaze from his to turn to Martin. "It's Stefan's cousin isn't it? Stefan told me his cousin was a witness in some very important prosecution. What happened? Does Stefan know?"

"I was told you were brilliant, Miss Lass. You live up to your reputation."

Ian freed his arm from her hold.

"Why now? The case has been open for weeks. What were you waiting for to step in? For the mob to confirm they outsmarted you? Two good men died and my best friend is in the hospital because of that bomb."

For the first time and to the blond detective's satisfaction, the agent seemed at a loss for words. Ian tamed an urge to snigger. He narrowed hard eyes at the scattered papers.

"You haven't answered Neve's question. What happened?"

Martin followed his stare. He brought the documents into a neat pile.

"We don't know for sure. I went to collect the new SA, but when we came back, the house was empty save for him."

He foraged through the photos then brandished one.

"This is typical Mafia' MO. One bullet in the back of the head. Clean, and efficient."

Neve winced. Ian digested the information in silence. Pieces of the puzzle were fitting together well. The Mafia wanted that witness and other FBI prospects to shut up. So they looked to tie loose ends. Stefan was the closest Beneto as of a family or so; a body in a park was a damned good warning to give him. One stone, two birds. Then, if that didn't work, you harmed the next person on line. He spun toward Neve. Martin preceded him.

"You need protection."

Apparently, the FBI had reached the same conclusion.

"Me?"

She seemed genuinely surprised. Ian gritted his teeth. She was too damned innocent to be a part of this, PI or not.

"Stefan didn't get a new identity just because he's a good sport. Damn it, Neve!"

"We will keep you out of sight until the judge–"

"No! I'm not relocating, not now, or ever. I worked too hard for what I have. Plus, you don't have any proof. It was probably just a break-in, you said so yourself, Ian…"

He grunted. "I never said that."

She scowled.

"I can't protect you 24/7."

"I'm not asking you to! I can take care of myself."

"Right. You did so well a couple of days ago."

Neve shot him a dark look. Martin folded his hands on the now closed folder.

"Miss Lass; I understand your reluctance, considering your family's history but–"

The threatening glare changed target in a flash of anger.

"My decision has nothing to do with my brother."

Neve chanced a glimpse in Ian's direction to find him staring back. She'd felt the change the moment it happened. Anger and resentment surged from his relentless stance. Tension crackled in between the trio. The federal agent yielded first.

"Very well. If you change your mind, here is my number. I would appreciate that you let me know about your associate's whereabouts too. Obviously, I expect your entire discretion regarding this conversation. Detective, I will inform your captain that the Bureau is taking charge of this case. Good day."

Martin exited the room, file in hand. Ian's mouth was merely more than a line. His eyes wanted to carve pieces out of her.

"Funny how it always goes back to your brother."

Self-preservation kicked in.

"It doesn't Ian; you make it so."

"Your brother killed my dad!"

Her voice hovered over a bottomless abyss.

"He didn't place that bomb!"

The horrid smell crushed her throat. She croaked, "I knew you were a jackass, I never imagined you were a heartless jerk too. What do you want me to say, Ian? That it was my fault? Fine! It was! It is! My brother made wrong choices because of me. He wanted me to have food, and a warm bed. He wanted me to be as happy as an orphan girl could be at seven!"

Her vision blurred at the edge. She refused to give in the tears and the heartache, the feeling of the last crumble of her innocence shattering. She wouldn't break, not in front of him.

"We were happy! We were together, we were a family. And then your mighty father came around. He convinced him that the only way to keep me really safe was to turn his cloak. So Mark did! He betrayed the wrong people and he died, and took your father with him! I'm sorry for that, but you're so unfair and bitter. Did you ever consider how it was for me? You still had your mother, and the rest of your relatives. I had no one left!"

Ian's face had darkened so his eyes fixed on her shone like topaz. The dam had broken and it was too late to contain the everlasting pain and the guilt.

"I was shipped from one elementary school to another until I was ten. It took four years for the Court to acknowledge my godfather as my guardian!"

Her anger trimmed into a snarl. His piercing gaze fired riots in the pit of her stomach. She paused to even her breathing. Ian crossed his arms over his chest.

"Feeling better?"

"You miserly, arrogant jerk!"

She launched herself at him, ready to claw his smirk out. He snatched her hand in midair. She thrashed to get free. He held tight. Her lips tightened, and her eyes were hot enough to vaporize lava. He ignored it.

"Except for those fly-swat abilities, are you armed?"

"What?"

His abrupt change of mood threw her off balance so she let him drag her out of the morgue. The surprised looks of the few people in the corridor embarrassed and riled her. She couldn't believe he didn't even bother to fight back. She braced herself for his next move. The moron was nothing but an arrogant, miserly jerk. If not for the risk of a public humiliation, she would.

They entered the precinct armory. Ian released her. Neve inhaled sharply. After the forbidden cleanliness of the examination room, the vague oily scent in the gun storage was almost welcoming. She put on a show of rubbing her wrist. He shrugged.

"So? Gun?"

"Yes. I have one. It's in the safe at the agency, a .357 Magnum."

"Useless. Tom!"

A tall languid man in uniform appeared from behind a cabinet. His hands were twisting a wipe around a barrel.

"I need a 9 millimeter Beretta. As short-barrel as you have."

The man nodded and padded in the cavern of shelves in the back.

"The Beretta is lighter, and at least it's a semi-automatic, not a revolver. The kick's minimal."

"You–"

The objection died on her lips when Ian stepped closer.

"I heard you. You made it damned impossible not to. But I'm not letting you out of here without protection. So take the gun and keep your nose clean for the time being. *Capice?*"

Completely baffled, Neve stared at him, signed the register and strode out.

Chapter 13

By the time Neve reached her office, she was boiling again. Ian had forced her to dig deep in memories and feelings she had worked hard to push aside. Embers from the past invaded her mind, still exquisitely hurtful.

One in particular scorched the back of her throat like inflamed sandpaper while she logged on her office computer. She saw herself coloring a crooked flower with her tongue tucked out in that special way children have. Mark was teasing her about the castle she had just finished, which was far too small for the two stick figures that represented them. She remembered the smell from the spaghetti sauce pot behind him, and the drawing, but not the kitchen itself. He always pressed fresh orange juice on Sunday mornings.

She wiped the wet scorch in her eyes and climbed the flight of steps. She barely made it inside her office before Terence hugged the inner doorjamb.

"Miss Neve, they're here."

Her keys escaped to crash on the floor. She snatched them up angrily.

"Who?"

The old man gave her a surprised and pained look.

"Well, the repair crew you asked for. I mentioned they were coming yesterday."

Neve flushed and flashed a quick smile, shouldering off her coat.

"Yes, I remember. Sorry, I'm a bit jumpy these days. Please tell them to come up."

The caretaker nodded stiffly and left.

The young woman glared at the deformed bump the Berretta made in her pocket. This was Ian's fault. It always was Ian's fault. He managed to make her feel inadequate and dour at every turn. She'd been a fool to accept working with him. She was Private. Bourque didn't really have the power to enroll her if she didn't want to. She accepted because she felt she had to prove herself, and it made it even worse.

She combed her fingers through her ponytail, tugging harder than necessary. The pinch cleared her mind a little.

"Miss?" a man in his fifties called, with a twenty-something man holding a toolbox behind him.

"We're here for an ill-fitting window."

Neve waved them in. Mail had piled up on her desk. So much for the electronic era. She started ruffling through commercial pamphlets and the mandatory bills while explaining, "It doesn't close correctly so strong winds flap it open."

"It's not as if we lack them this season, eh?"

Neve glanced up at the drawl before returning to her task. Encouraged by that clear mark of interest, the man lengthened on the explanations.

"In these old buildings, the frames deformed with age, so the bottom case tends to go unaligned. The shutter dog crooks, paint stiffens the latch and the pintles, and hop, you're screwed, easy as pie. See that hook here? It's disjointed."

A teeth-breaking groan added to the speech when he pulled the window open.

"Miss, maybe you'll want to dim your heating system a bit while we work, eh? No need to waste coal warming the birds, as my *ole wan* used to say."

She sighed, and did as he said.

*

The chains squeaked in protest. A faint stampede echoed that confirmed Kermit was hiding under the sofa.

Ian backhanded his fist in the punching bag again. Without protecting straps, his knuckles hurt like hell. He punched the leather bag again. The pain magnified up his fists.

The pressure in his chest was still there. What did she call him? A 'heartless jackass' and a 'miserly jerk'. Yeah that was an accurate way to describe him. He never considered how she'd lived after the attack. *Hook. Jab. Punch.* How she survived. *Hook. Hook. Punch.* Truth was he hadn't known, because he never cared to look. The punching bag bounced back.

The truth… Ian paused to snigger at himself. The truth squashed him into a pulp. And he deserved it. He deserved every insult she had thrown his way, and then some. A renewed urge to break something rushed up from the pit of his stomach.

His cell phone shrilled on the nightstand.

"Braich."

'Ian, it's Lauren.'

"Can it wait?"

'Wow, are you all right? You sound–'

"No, I'm not all right, Lauren. I'm an imbecile and a coward, so unless–"

'Been playing Truth or Dare with Neve again, have you?'

Ian fought the need to hurl the damned phone against the wall. His hand throbbed when he tightened his grip.

'Are you still at the station?'

"No, I'm home. Why?"

Lauren neglected to answer his question, as always.

'Good, so you can talk. I received a call from Caleb. Never mind how he got-'

Ian uncorked a bottle of water and gulped half of it down. The bed cracked under his weight.

'Ian, are you listening?'

"Yes, I'm listening. Caleb'd been naughty, then he called you and now you're calling me. So what's the pun?"

'Screw it, Ian. It's about the grenade. The simulations... Never mind the details now-' Her voice itched. He straightened up. Lauren never spared anyone the technical details; never. He focused on her voice again. *'...blast on the decreasing arc.'*

He'd missed enough to lose her meaning. The blanks he tried to fill had his blood run cold.

"Come again?"

'The grenade couldn't come down at such an angle from a direct throw, it's impossible, Ian. The angle was way too steep. It was on a descending curve.'

"They were targeting the second floor."

The forensic lab was on the second floor; Lauren's lab. He jumped on his feet.

"Damn it. Goddammit! Lauren, put Luke on."

'I'm here, Ian.'

"Call Bourque; Lauren needs protection, and–"

'I don't think it was for my sister or Caleb, Ian. She was not supposed to be there last weekend.'

"She came in to finish God knows what for Neve. Shit! Shit! Shit!"

Ian grabbed his holster. The safety catch clicked back into place with a round chambered in the Glock. Kermit who had tiptoed inside the bedroom torpedoed past him under the bed with a very un-feline squeal.

*

Even with the heater pushed to the maximum, the tip of her nose was burning cold. Neve sighed. Her impromptu guests announced they'd be 'all done in five minutes' for the seventh time. She'd considered dismissing them for the last hour, but at this point, it made no sense. Between the cold and the constant noise, she felt numb, completely drained of energy.

A sharp knock on the door coerced her out of her torpor.

"Come in!"

She regretted the invitation as soon as the door cringed open. The familiar silhouette on the threshold belonged to the last person she wanted to see at the moment. To add insult to injury, the opening created a chilly draft worse than the previous whiffs she had endured.

Ian used the plastic bag in his hands as a shield.

"I've come in peace... And I have soup."

She recognized the logo on the bags from the small Asian take-out shop at the corner. The workers glanced at him then started whispering. Ian stepped inside without waiting for an invitation.

"Why don't you go and eat in the stairs while I keep watch in the igloo?"

"That's all right, Detective. Those gentlemen here promised they'll be finished in about five minutes."

The whispers died right away. Ian knitted his brows at the title but for once, he kept his mouth shut. And the mention had the exact effect she was hoping for. Neve barely had the time to unpack two small boxes in addition to the wonton soup before the window magically closed.

"All done."

"We'll see."

Ian yanked the knob hard once, then shouldered the frame. The bolt hold tight. Neve preferred to work the latch on and off a few times before she declared herself satisfied. The exercise set the tip of her fingers on fire. Her signature on the receipt looked crooked. The nuisance was out of her office before she could even thank them. Ian grinned.

"Guess it'll hold."

"I do hope so... Hum, this is fabulous..."

The fragrant hot liquid coated her palate and her throat with heat. Ian uncapped his own bowl with an awkward nod.

"Look, Neve... I... About earlier..."

"This," she touched his sleeve pointing at the take-out spread between them, "is nice. So don't ruin it."

Neve tempered the jibe with a smile. Every degree the heater labored to deliver brightened her mood. Plus, roasted duck was one of her favorites. Really, no reason to talk and ruin everything. She sensed he was about to insist, but decided against it. Allowing her the last word twice in less than five minutes, that was certainly a first.

They ate in silence, until Ian pointed at the mess on her desk with his chopstick.

"Did you have time to work on that list we talked about the other day?"

Unsettled by the question, Neve pecked at the bottom of her box for crumbles of duck.

"Not really. With all that happened..."

Ian backed in his seat to stretch his arms on the header. Neve shot him an awry look and stood to collect the remains of their dinner. He caught her meaning and straightened up, but made no move to take his leave.

"I'd like to have this list."

"But the FBI said–" she frowned mid-sentence. "Why are you here exactly? And don't serve me anything about making amends."

His smile was forced and flickered within seconds as he held the bag.

"I don't like loose ends."

She wanted to ask what loose ends, but something in his gaze stopped her. Accepting some help to clean up wasn't like forgiving him, right?

"All right. We can use the billing list, but we'll have to check each file separately, I don't remember every detail by heart," Neve lied. She was sure that she would remember the basics of each case. Instinct told her that Ian was hiding something from her; she wanted to know what.

*

Her power of concentration was incredible, Ian decided. They'd been going through those files for hours and she hadn't budged an inch. His neck ached from being bent over miles of paper. His brain had stopped registering what he had before his eyes a long time ago. The only concession Neve had given to the world around her was the messy bun she'd made with her hair so they stopped falling into her face while her eyes noticed every line.

His gaze followed a rebel curl along the curve of her shoulder. The heater was still running at full blast. Why they had chosen to ditch some layers rather than turning it down, he had no clue. Maybe it had to do with stopping what they were doing. He squinted at the hem of her sleeve.

"Did I do that?"

"Hum?"

He leaned forward but stopped short before brushing the greenish mark on her upper arm. Guilt tasted foul in his mouth. He regretted agreeing to that sparring session the other day; and taking her down this morning. He regretted a lot of things. It would take more than Chinese take-out to correct his wrongs.

Ian hid behind his customary smirk.

"Do you realize we've just exploded our record? We've been alone together for about three hours, and we're still civil with each other."

She stopped tapping her pen to her jaw to finally look up at him. The continuous drum had irritated the skin between her neck and her earlobe. The urge to lean forward and soothe the red mark unsettled him. Ian stood to put some distance between them.

"I could do with a break; and some caffeine, given you apparently want to go through the whole bunch of files tonight. Do you have a coffee maker somewhere?"

Neve jolted up. "Sorry. I haven't realized it was that late."

She chewed her upper lip with an abashed look on her face.

"Stefan complains all the time that I don't know when to stop."

Ian raised one eyebrow, grinning up his sleeve.

"I wasn't. Complaining, I mean. But of course if you insist on an apology…"

Neve blushed furiously. There was a subtle change in his attitude. His lopsided grin seemed the same. His eyes still tried to bore her into the ground. His hands were flexing by his side as if he were bored to death and couldn't wait to get away. And yet… Yet there was something in his voice that softened the lecherous jest. A different glint lit his pupils.

She cleared her throat and then moved to stand.

"We should call it a night. I'll finish this tomorrow and let you know of what I–"

Her legs trembled at the sudden effort. Ian reached for her hand to help her up before she found the strength to finish her sentence. Neve bit her inner cheek when the contact sent sparks up her spine. She teased to break the intimacy growing fast around them.

"Manners, Braich? I'm impressed…"

"I do my best to hide them. Can't let women get the wrong idea, can I?"

She laughed.

"Your secret is safe with me."

Ian returned the smirk, and picked up his jacket on the back of the couch while she put the alarm on.

"I'll walk you back to your place."

She bobbed her head, amused by the old-fashioned machismo, and deep down grateful for the offer. Exhaustion teased her eyes to close.

At 11:20 p.m., the street was empty. Ian straightened up his collar. After the tropical warm in her office, winter bit hard. Neve walked for a few yards in the general direction of her car, then turned. His dumbfounded look seemed to amuse her senseless. Neve stepped aside spreading both arms wide, like the beaming hostess of some TV show.

"1021C, Harmon Street. Home sweet home."

Ian tousled his hair with one hand. Slowly, she was learning his mannerisms: the way he stretched his arms above his head and linked his hands over his nap when he was in deep thought, or the embarrassed ruffle of hair. Neve wished she could stop noticing those details. He yawned in his elbow, and rolled one shoulder backward, squeezing the tired muscles with one hand. She unlocked the door, giving him a peek of a minuscule hall before she started up the flight of steps. He followed, curious to

115

know where she lived. The first floor was cast in shadows. The keys jingled in her hand.

The light created a halo around her frame. Ian coughed before his brain started playing with a world of fascinating possibilities. Her smiles held too many mysteries to take at once.

"I'll just make sure everything's in order."

With more rumpling, his hair spiked in every direction. Neve smiled before she caught herself. Her cheeks took a delicate shade of pink as she spoke.

"Aren't you overreacting a bit?"

"I insist."

"As you wish."

He eyed the loft-like living room open on the kitchen, with its gigantic windows, and the two small corridors leading to the sleeping quarters, one of each side of the apartment. Did he know Stefan was gone already?

"The bedroom's this way."

Ian's hand shot up to scratch his scalp as his eyes widened a bit then narrowed on her. The funny feeling in the pit of her stomach flared.

"I mean..."

Neve put her keys down before they escaped her fingers. She was still shaky from her misadventure. She seriously wouldn't consider... Ian waited for her to finish her sentence, staring.

'The hell with it'.

Her hand curled around his neck and helped his mouth down to hers.

This time, Ian didn't hesitate. He parted her lips and conquered her mouth in one stroke. The strong, confident woman who made a point of resisting him at every turn melted into the kiss, magically transformed into a cloud of softness. The kiss simmered, languid and greedy all at once. One hand hooked in her hair to forbid some improbable escape. Ian explored her back with the other, pushing fabric out of his way.

Neve sighed against his lips. His shoulders trembled when her fingers flitted by them to assault his shirt. Ian muttered something rough and broken, his breath hot against her throat. She arched back to kiss him again, and they danced together across the room, lips locked, hands clumsy; needy.

They avoided hitting the bedroom doorframe by a hair. The bed appeared out of nowhere in a waltz of hot caresses and falling clothes. When she stepped off the pool her pants formed on the floor, Ian drowned in the sight of glorious pale skin and midnight blue lace.

Chapter 14

Ian tugged at the mass under his head.

"Why do you have so many pillows?"

Neve whined sleepily. She shifted in the bed to bury her face between the fluffy bumps.

"Because..."

The answer or the lack of it made him smile. Ian shifted in the bed to look at the woman by his side. Her hair was undone, contrasting with her pale skin. The glow spilling through the curtains coated her body with light, like an airy satin, made her tawny eyes brighter. She looked beautiful.

Uncomfortable with the thought, Ian rolled on his back.

"What did Bourque mean about the Academy?"

The question caused her back to stiffen under waves of silken hair. It nagged at him ever since his captain had mentioned it. Maybe it wasn't the wisest subject but the others he had in mind, Lauren's warning, or their respective past, didn't provide safer paths.

"You never struck me as the 'talk-after-sex' type."

Frustration stirred deep inside him at her tone, very familiar and definitely unwelcomed.

"I didn't think that *you* would take *me* to bed, of all people."

The retort echoed nastily in the quiet room. He wanted to bang his head on the headboard, but the crowding pillows denied him. He stifled a groan. Neve pushed up, preparing to flee or worse, chase him away, so he leaned toward her to brush her shoulder.

"That came out wrong..."

He trailed off, distracted by the curves under his palm. His hand feathered her back in the same way he used to tame Kermit's feline moods. Ian moved closer to scatter kisses from her shoulder blade to her spine. He relished the delicate flavor of her skin, sweet as honey with a hint of cinnamon.

Neve relaxed, her eyes fluttering closed again. Ian landed one last butterfly kiss on her arm before he plowed on, "So? Why did you leave?"

"Why do you ask?"

Her voice lowered to a suspicious growl. He hesitated to press the matter further, and let himself swaddle in the blissful daze that lingered in the shadows. Curiosity won.

"You're good. You could have finished in the top ten, chose your deployment."

She didn't want to think about the file on the captain's desk. Neve stretched her arms under her pillow, bringing it over his shoulder. Ian whisked the obstruction out of his way. She nestled against his upper arm, resigned to rest without the cushion.

"It's complicated."

His fingers followed the path his mouth had taken minutes ago, drawing slow figure eights down the back of her arm before it slipped around her elbow.

"I'm good at complicated."

The ghost of a smile softened her frown. He waited, his hand still playing scales up and down her back as if she were a beautiful piano. She scrutinized the side of his face an instant before she started murmuring. The memory seemed too grim for more than a whisper.

"Someone stole the partial tests, and replaced them with fakes. The committee noticed the substitution only after the exams took place when they review the scores. I aced them all. Every single test. So they thought it was me."

"You would never have done that."

Neve gave him another thoughtful look. Then she snuggled closer, so her head was tucked in the crook of his shoulder under his chin. Ian welcomed her in his arms, still brushing her hip in subtle encouragement.

"I had the opportunity, because I worked with the staff; and my family had a 'reputation' in forgery."

His hand stopped for a breath, before it went on with its lulling pattern.

"Given my godfather was on the board, I was offered the possibility to quit, without disgrace."

Ian grunted. "Why didn't you fight?"

Cocooned in his arms, remembering wasn't that hard.

"I didn't want to embarrass my godfather. He was already ill, and he had too much on his plate already with the Isabella Stewart Gardner's art heist. He always refused to leave it alone, even…"

She paused, thinking about her uncle's last days, emaciated in his bed, surrounded by papers and photographs, while the tumor in his brain killed him slowly. The images of those heated looks he gave her every time she wanted to take his mind off the famous mystery still hurt, even two years later. In the end, she had given up trying. He had died doing what he loved most. For that she was grateful. Neve sighed.

"I just took the offer and quit. A couple of months later, they caught the thief. They offered to let me finish my training, even send a very nice letter of excuses… I would not have gone back anyway. I was already working with Lawrence. When he retired, I bought his practice, and kept going."

Ian kissed her forehead lightly.

"It's still unfair. I don't understand why…"

Neve smiled in his neck. The righteous part of him rebelled at the injustice, even if the victim was someone he… She struggled to find the proper verb. He called her beautiful while they made love, and said she was brilliant while they worked together. He also had called her a mule, and countless other things. Ian stretched, pulling her close again as she backed to give him space.

"You would have made a good cop. You have the instinct."

She smiled, for real this time. Only hours ago, she would have chastised herself for being pleased because he complimented her. But who said she couldn't indulge herself until dawn?

"Well, all things considered, I don't regret my decision. Besides, the pay is better."

Ian snorted. Neve teased, "I can make my own hours."

His slow grin grew to match hers.

"I don't have to fill requests in triple for a lab analysis."

"I still resent that."

"And I have the privilege to upset the best cops in the country."

Ian's carnal smile bared his teeth. He flipped them over on the mattress so he had the upper hand. His nose grazed hers.

"I wouldn't say upset, exactly."

Neve arched under him, inviting him closer.

"Did I mention your name?"

Their lips brushed, speeding her heartbeat.

"I *am* the best, Neve, and you know it."

He swallowed her reply with a kiss. Her last coherent thought was that one of these days, she would give his ego a serious wound. One day. Just not now…

*

Ian woke up with a start. The beautiful woman by his side stirred, her eyes fighting to open.

"What?.."

"There's someone here."

Neve yawned, glaring back at the red 6 glowing on the clock.

"Must be Stefan…"

"No, I don't think so."

When the Feds got you in a safe house, the only leave you got was to go to Court. Neve moved to get up, but Ian stopped her.

"I'll check. Go back to sleep."

He pulled his shorts up, fishing his gun in another bundle on the floor. Neve pushed the sheets in turn. She blinked as he took the safety off.

"What are you doing?"

"Just a precaution. Stay here."

"I–"

A crash followed a muffled curse. Neve grabbed the first piece of clothing she could find on the floor. Ian padded to the door. Fortunately, it didn't creak when he pushed it aside for a better view of the living room. The curtains were half drawn, so the early light made it hard to distinguish anything more than dark blurs. He squinted, his eyes searching for the intruder.

Neve's warm body appeared at his back. Ian growled, "I told you to stay in bed."

"I'm not going to wait while you raid my living room," she answered in the same urgent, hushed tone. A

123

shadow moved ahead. Neve twitched to pass before him. Ian circled her waist with one arm, pulling her back. She stalled. As far as he could tell, she wore nothing but his shirt. The young man changed tactics, nudging her hip through the fabric.

"You could get hurt. Please, stand back…"

Her nostrils flared. She opened her mouth, closed it for half a second, and retorted.

"Don't even think this is going to work."

Yet she did nothing to escape the caress or pass by him again. Ian returned his attention to the other room. The mouse noises started again, farther inside the apartment. One door squealed with a brief flash of light. The fridge, he guessed. Maybe it was Stefan, who had escaped the FBI's watch. Or maybe it wasn't. He prepared to move forward…

The bright light nearly blinded him. Cutlery crashed on the counter top and the floor. The metallic screech racked his nerves. The form in front of him was definitely too small to be Stefan. Ian took aim.

"Freeze!"

"Ian, don't!"

Neve jumped forward, abandoning the light switch. Her right hand tried to press his arm down, the other extended as a peace offering toward the tiny silhouette in the kitchen.

The strange girl's parka and baggy pants had seen better days. She couldn't be more than thirteen or fourteen, and skinny in that painful way only homeless teens could be. Dirty blonde curls framed her cat face. Burning, suspicious dark eyes watched him under thick lashes, taking in his bare chest and Neve's shirt. The girl snorted.

"Didn't know stopping by for a sandwich would turn into an X-rated show."

Ian refused to yield to Neve's soothing, his Glock still pointed forward.

"Who are you?"

She ignored the question, eyeing Neve with a mix of shock and reproach.

"You said I could drop by anytime."

Neve sighed. The hand she had wrapped around his forearm slowly withdrew. He put the gun aside, making a show of putting the safety back on. Neve rolled her eyes slightly at the display.

"You could have called first, Mouse…"

The girl offered a prim, almost ladylike sneer.

"Not sure you would have picked up the phone. It seemed you were quite… occupied."

Ian growled in response, earning himself a glare from the beautiful brunette, and a sneer from the scrawny figure challenging him.

"Can't say I blame you, though. He's a nice morsel, as far as I can see."

Ian cleared his throat again. This time, Neve was too flushed to scowl at him. He crossed his arms across his chest.

"And you are?…"

"Who's asking?"

"Ian Braich, VPD."

"Can't say it rings a bell."

The girl skipped toward the couch, her plate in one hand, clearly unimpressed.

He had spent enough time on the force to recognize trouble when he saw it. This girl had it flashing over her head like neon. Neve moved forward before he could press the matter further.

"If you are hungry, you'll have a decent breakfast, not–" she eyed the pile of food within the bread, from pickles to ham and what looked suspiciously like bananas, "that. Go scrub yourself clean. I'll bring you clothes."

"But–"

"No but. Now, Madeline."

The teen pursed her lips, sulking. The eye contest lasted for a few seconds, then Mouse/Madeline sighed. She put her plate down on the coffee table. Another glare from Neve had her pick it up and bring the bizarre sandwich to the kitchen. Ian wanted to laugh. He smothered his smile, so as not to spoil the little authority she seemed to have on the grubby stray cat. He also had the nagging feeling that as soon as this one was out of sight, it would be his turn to get flogged.

It didn't take that long. Neve jabbed two fingers into his bare chest.

"Did you have to be that harsh?"

"*I* was harsh? That… girl picked your lock in the middle of the night so that she could empty your fridge!"

She shrugged, stepping away. Shaking his head in disbelief, Ian tried to reconcile the dove-like woman he had made love to a few hours ago with the distant figure moving around the appliances in the kitchen. The disgusting sandwich found its way to the garbage can.

"I don't mind. At least it means she'll be out of the streets for a couple of hours."

The edge in her voice made him pause. A part of his brain wondered why it mattered. Another wanted to take her back to bed, away from the world, and its ugly reality. She chose for him.

"I wish I could offer breakfast to you too, but she won't feel at ease if there's a cop around."

His ego shouted that he'd been there first. Ian stood his ground.

"Who is she?"

"I don't really know. She calls herself Mouse, but her first name is Madeline. She never told us her last name."

He supposed 'us' included Stefan. She opened the fridge to take out eggs, ham, and cheese.

"It doesn't matter anyway. We spent time interviewing homeless people when a woman hired us to find her father. He had gone AWOL from the establishment that treated him for Alzheimer's."

He remembered reading about that in her folders. The previous evening felt billions of years ago. Neve oiled the pan.

"Mouse lurked around the people we talked to. She tried to lift Stefan's wallet, but he caught her. We didn't press charges and in exchange, she pops in the agency from time to time when she hears things that she thinks we want to know."

Ian flexed his hands, unwilling and drawn to stay at the same time. The eggs sizzled in the pan.

"You realize she could be responsible for…"

Neve glowered at him above her shoulder. He trailed off but refused to back off. He was entitled to ask. The urchin had had the opportunity to make a move on the agency. Motives were plenty. She picked the lock, and her accomplice had assaulted Neve when she showed up.

The named woman was staring at him, an eye on her cooking. He chose another attack angle.

"What can she possibly know that interests you?"

Neve pursed her lips. The forbidding glare tore away the last of the intimate veil the night had slung above them. Ian inhaled once, and then turned away. Picking up his abandoned gun, he backed to her bedroom.

On the other side of the apartment, the waterfall stopped. Neve took her pan off the stove and entered her room to search the bottom drawer of her dresser. She sounded almost sheepish when she noticed he was zipping up his jeans.

"I promised her fresh clothes."

He didn't acknowledge her, still gathering up his clothes scattered on the floor to dress. Ian pulled his jacket collar up to his neck. The fabric swished on his undershirt. He did his best not to look at the unmade bed between them. She stood with an uncertain look that twisted his insides into knots.

"Ian?"

He'd be damned if he let her think he minded being cast aside for a guttersnipe. He wasn't totally sure why he minded himself. The women he dated in the last couple of years didn't look so lovely in his shirt.

"I forgot to feed the cat. Catch up later."

He escaped the apartment without another word.

Chapter 15

Neve tucked her laptop behind her seat then loaded her bag on the back. After her disastrous morning, she'd welcome her client's request for an in-person presentation of her conclusions to the settlement committee in Boston with open arms. Normally, she preferred hitting New York rather than the Walking City, especially in winter. But home was too quiet without Stefan. And she was not in a hurry to face Ian. So Boston it was. She caught herself burying her nose in the sheets when she changed the bedding. A change of air was definitely in order.

Neve engaged her car left on the ramp to reach I-91N. Tolls would go to her bill. She tuned in a traffic station on the radio then changed her mind. The four lanes of the interstate were nearly empty. She screened broadcasts for something to sing along with, so her mind would stop wandering a few hours back in time.

The last thing she needed was romanticizing her relationship with Ian. They simply scratched an itch; explored the fire that raged whenever they faced each other. Maybe nestled against him in bed, she'd let the tiny part of her that still believed in fairy tales and happy endings tweet louder. She blamed tiredness and daze. But it was daylight now; she was wide awake, and she had too much common sense to start fantasizing. Their common past basked in too much qualm and anger for anything tender to bloom anyway.

Neve focused her attention on the road. The night wind had swept the asphalt clean to leave it a soft pale gray that hurt the eye. She fished for her sunglasses in the glove compartment.

Her presentation was scheduled for the next morning. She'd had little time to prepare, but it didn't worry her. Her investigation was thorough, the conclusions backed by facts and solid reasoning. She couldn't say the same about Madeline's accusations. She suspected the girl had made up yet another story about dirty cops to protect her pride, unwilling to admit the bitter cold had chased her away from the streets. Or maybe she wanted to make her feel guilty about Ian. His fault, again. What need did he have to boast about his badge in front of Mouse? It'd taken months for Neve to tame the lost girl, who distrusted grown-ups, male authority in general, and cops in particular with a passion. He should have known better. The man was impossible. Which was exactly why she didn't want to think about him. What she wanted was a nice weekend in Boston, including a long, exhausting visit to Newbury Street.

Her cell phone belled but she ignored it, and pumped up the volume of the radio.

Two hours later, stuck in the afternoon rush hour on the Mass Pike, Neve wondered why she had chosen to drive from Vallon instead of using the Acela Express train. She didn't even plan to use the car after her meeting. Her hotel was in downtown Boston in the Theatre District, a stone's throw away from shops, restaurants, and museums.

A clearing appeared between a two-level bus and a hesitant car, so Neve wrenched the wheel to change lanes. A concert of horns escorted her. She waved her hand in apology and hustled toward the exit.

A small sign advertised Albany Street. She brushed the breaks to signal the car behind her to back off. The white high beams blinded her for a second before the car closed the distance again. Neve hissed between her teeth. She didn't know Boston that well, and she hated having vehicles breathing down her neck, especially if she was lost. The nasty feeling she was heading the wrong way grew stronger. The street was narrow by Bostonian standards, with dark buildings and empty parking lots.

Swearing under her breath, she squinted at the panels, looking for direction. Snow and frost covered the labels so that she couldn't read the names. She hit the brakes at the next crossing, skidding slightly on the asphalt. Her tail did the same. Neve swerved. The yellowish glow from lamp posts reflected on the windshield, so her scowl was lost. Typical behavior. See a foreign plate, and courtesy be damned.

She set her car in gear again, aiming for the patch of light a hundred yards again. Her elbow brushed the command for the automatic unlock of the doors. The click frayed her nerves.

"Stop fretting," she chastised herself out loud. "You're overreacting because the last few days were hell. Handymen are just handymen, and this asshole doesn't know how to drive. So stop. It."

The sermon was useless. Every few seconds, she glimpsed at the shadow in the mirror. The way it moved behind her sent a shiver down her spine. They were the only moving vehicles in the street, so she changed lanes to let it pass. The car imitated her. Neve straightened up in her seat. Her foot flirted with the accelerator, finally putting some distance between them.

Not for long. The blaze became Massachusetts Avenue. Her pulse skyrocketed. The traffic light blinked between yellow and red. White light filled her mirror. On an impulse, she crushed the accelerator and skidded right on the avenue. The blood pounding in her ears dulled the shrills behind her. She didn't dare glimpse behind.

*

Some of the people boarding the settlement committee she had met in the past. Even though they were not happy with the results of her investigation, the presentation and period of questions stayed friendly.

"So, Miss Lass, if I understand you correctly, you found anomalies, but none of the actual destruction of the piece insured by the fire, or its authenticity?"

"Yes, Sir."

"Your report here mentions ancient bronze," a woman said. The pearls around her dry neck mirrored the green of her tweed dress.

"Yes, Ma'am. The laboratory concluded the porcelain plate was placed on that bronze piece, for support."

"We have nothing of the sort on the list that corroborates that hypothesis. I don't see why Mr. Goblin would have insured an eighteenth-century porcelain plate, but not antique bronze."

"I asked myself the same question, Ma'am," answered Neve. "The technician also explained that her assertion of bronze was hypothetical; the fragments we gathered were heavily damaged by the fire, so she gave her results a forty-eight percent chance of probability."

Pearl-woman nodded, resuming her reading. Neve's handler, a man in his fifties with a soft spot for beer stood up at the end of the table.

"Well, Miss Lass, in the name of this committee, I thank you for your time and your excellent job, as usual. Will you join us for lunch?"

"Thank you, Sir, but I have to decline. I have other commitments."

"Very well, then. We'll stay in touch."

The other commitments were in name only. While her taxi driver tried to convince her to go out for drinks, she had spotted a sign toward the Isabella Stewart Gardner Museum. Despite the hard memories of her godfather the place brought back, Neve decided to go and visit the collection once again.

Being Thursday early afternoon, the museum was nearly empty. She hit the Café G first, and calmed her grumbling stomach with fresh salmon and gnocchi while planning her tour. After a long internal argument, she skipped dessert and went directly to the second floor. The gorgeous Veronese and Titian Art on the third floor she left aside for another visit. Neve strolled through the early Italian rooms, attracted as usual to the amazing tapestries.

She remembered long hours spent in front of the Flemish pieces of needlepoints. The colors, beige, soft blue, red and forest green mesmerized her. The portrait of Michael bringing down the dragon made her smile. Probably that was how Ian saw himself.

"Highly significant, don't you think, Miss Lass?"

Neve turned around with a start.

"Do I know you?"

A card slipped inside her hand, announcing Charles Books from the Criminal Division.

What do you want? She pressed her lips hard to stop the question from gushing out. She didn't care for anyone spoiling her weekend. Why would an ADA have to be here and introduce himself? The car that scared her last night... Neve glowered, her pleasant mood dissolving fast, through caution laced annoyance. Books declared, "I like this painting, but the Dutch Room holds much more impressive pieces. Shall we?"

She had little choice but to follow. The room was a wonder of gold and green empire wall paper. The numerous windows gave it space, despite the incredible concentration of paintings and objects on display. The snow gave an eerie glow to the Italian furniture. Neve stole a glance at her unwelcomed escort. His smile was too broad for her taste.

Far from impressed by the extraordinary silver boxes, or the hanging portraits of duchesses, queens and doctors, the attorney led them directly in front of the empty frames.

Neve swallowed, memories adding to wariness. She remembered well her last visit. Her godfather had spent two hours lecturing her about how the museum had chosen to keep those frames empty, as a reminder of the stolen masterpieces. Her heart pounded aggressively at her ribs. The 1990 St. Patrick day theft had despoiled her of the last of her family, her godfather obsessing more and more by it with the years, until he died… She had planned to come in here step by step, almost without thinking, in hopes the loss appeared less blatant. Books destroyed that. Anger bubbled up.

"What do you want from me?"

Her tone hit the same wall of amused indifference Ian had some days ago. All of a sudden, she understood the detective's frustration very well.

"I was hoping for some friendly conversation. May I suggest coffee? I was told Café G is quite well known."

If she had wanted a free drink, she would have acknowledged the unsubtle compliments of her taxi driver.

"No, thank you. You followed me here, and I don't appreciate the intrusion."

If she ever discovered he had anything to do with that car… The patient smile grated on her nerves.

"Straight to the point, then. Very well. What can you tell me about your brother?"

The question deflated her. A guide shepherded a group of retired people inside the room, and started explaining about Isabella Stewart's love for that particular room. The lady had entertained guests here at the turn of the twentieth century. She forced herself to return a polite nod from an elderly woman with snow-white hair and a Red Sox jersey.

"I don't see what I can tell you. All I remember is a tall guy who helped me with math homework and watched cartoons with me."

"I'm sorry for your loss."

Like hell he was. He wanted something from her, though she couldn't fathom what. Mouse's dislike of the species suddenly felt very right. The only interest anyone from his office could have in her brother was linked to his extra-curricular activities. They didn't care about him, or her; the why behind frauds and deceits. And even if the man in his too-crisp suit watching her expectantly had cared, she could have said nothing. She discovered Mark's *profession* only as a teen; orphanages didn't talk about adult business with their wards, and her godfather had made sure she heard nothing until she was old enough to understand. By then, all traces of his misdeeds and his clients were long gone.

Neve squared her shoulders and met Books' eyes without a blink.

"I was seven when he died. I don't know anything about his business or his associates. The little we had was absorbed by the system."

They rented a furnished apartment. What the police hadn't seized fit in her My Little Pony pink suitcase. Her godfather had salvaged a couple of photos of her parents, small replicas of British monuments and a Simon and Garfunkel anthology album. She swallowed the lump in her throat. Coming to the museum had been a mistake. It seemed that was the only thing she did these days. Books stared a moment longer then stepped back.

"Of course. Thank you for your time. In case we don't see each other again, I wish you the best of luck."

The guide had moved in the front of the empty frames, and recited the list of the stolen art pieces that disappeared in 1990. Neve spun on her heels, and exited the room as fast as she could, pride be damned.

"A Vermeer, three Rembrandt canvases, five Degas sketches, a Chinese bronze beaker–"

The list reverberated endlessly behind her. She didn't look back.

Chapter 16

"So you failed, once again."

Useless scumbags, idiotic and incompetent. The man pulled at the wrists of his shirt, smoothing the creases of his sleeves. Idiocy he could live with. Idiocy had allowed him to navigate the thin line of deception for years. But to tolerate incompetence? Never.

One of the rats in front of him went on with pitiful excuses.

"She never left the place, not for a minute. We couldn't approach the computer with her breathing down our neck! And when she finally receded so that we had some space, her boyfriend came up."

"You never said she was doing a cop!" chirped the other.

He forced himself to inhale quietly. The air reeked of rotten meat, the odor enhanced by the sharp cold. The silence seemed to breathe courage into the hit men.

"What about our payment?"

"Where is my grenade launcher?"

The *cafflers* crossed him, and sold the military equipment to God knows who, and hand-pitched their explosive at the station. Without the launcher, they had missed the laboratory. Two cops were dead. He had taken big risks to get the weapon, cashing in old favors. Then they messed up copying Lass' hard-drive at her office. So he'd been forced to step in again, instead of managing the case from afar. Two mistakes and twice the risk for himself.

"What do we do now? If they look into us…"

He heard the tentative threat and lifted a finger.

"Clean up your mess. I don't care to know how. And don't seek me again. I'll call you."

*

Neve sighed as she contemplated the mess on the back seat. A closer parking spot would have been nice, considering the number of bags that she had to haul up. Oh well, she'd pick half of them now, her laptop and duffle bag, and then come back for the rest after lunch. Her stomach growled in approval of the plan.

She stepped on the sidewalk. Neve repressed a shiver, leaning forward to grab as many bags as she could. Her muscles protested when she straightened up with her arms full. She huffed. A second trip on this ice floe? No, thank you. She'd take everything at once and spend the rest of the afternoon relaxing in front of Hallmark movies.

Her breath came out in white puffs as she heaved toward the door. She unlocked it like a contortionist, one hip pushing the jamb open while she held some bags in place with her elbow pressed to her side, some handles caught between her teeth, others sawing at her wrists.

So maybe she had overdone herself in the shopping department. So what? She did need new slacks; and blouses. And new boots. The gold and red sandals were to die for, even though she would need to wait four months to wear them. And they complemented that dress she had bought last year just fine.

Neve stumbled inside then kicked the door closed. The package under her arm quivered. She pressed her elbow to keep it in place, fighting gravity. The landing at the top looked like Nirvana. Two more strides and she dropped everything on the couch, laptop included.

"Thank God…"

The door whined, immediately followed by a bang. The first step of the stairs creaked. Neve spun on her heels just in time to see a dark head run up the stairs. The Beretta was too far, locked away in her nightstand. Her heart in the throat, she grabbed the ugly white owl on the floor and swung it.

*

The abrupt chirp sneaked into his daze. Ian groaned as cool air wormed under the covers to nip at his skin. The alarm clock marked a few minutes after 11 a.m. He had taken the night shift and went to bed a little after six.

Kermit protested when he dislodged him from his side to forage the side table. The phone resumed its angry rant. He squinted at the name on the screen.

"Neve? What's the matter? Where are you?"

His head and the rest of his body felt as if he had been rolled run over by a bus. Twice.

"I… I think it would be better if you come over. I can't explain over the phone. Can you come to my place?"

Ian flapped off the covers, definitely awake.

"I'll be there in twenty."

*

Neve blinked.

139

The man rubbing the back of his head looked a bit like Stefan. He was about the same height, with broader shoulders and what she guessed was a more confident stance, at least when he was not lying prostrate on the floor. This one kept his hair cut short, and was grayed at the temples. He also needed a shave.

The stranger did look like Stefan, just more… Everything. He grinned, and she realized she was staring. Neve tightened her grip on the vase.

"Who are you? What are you doing here?"

He crouched as if to stand up. She fetched her guard a little higher.

"Maybe you could lower that thing before you do something you'll regret?"

"Answer my questions first! Who are you?"

"Nick. Nicholas Beneto. I think you cracked my skull with that thing…"

Cracked skull or not, he moved like a big cat, and the next thing she knew her weapon was in his hands. Neve yelped and jumped out of reach. The drawer where she kept the Beretta was too far away. Why hadn't she reached for it instead of calling Ian? She wasn't a damsel in distress who needed rescuing. She could handle herself. She'd been trained for these kinds of situations! But training didn't take place in her home; it felt like a violation. As if nowhere was safe anymore. She'd been assaulted in her office, and now her home…

Neve hated the way her heart pumped in her chest; bile churned in her stomach. She crept away, dilated eyes on her assailant. He put the vase on the floor then straightened up with his palms open in a display of good will. His smile showed too many teeth to be reassuring.

"I'm not going to hurt you… Please, calm down... Stefan said I could stay here for a while."

"Stefan?"

"Yes, Stefan, my cousin."

"Oh my God, you're... We thought you were dead!"

The man, Nick, stood on the other side of the table, looking sheepish.

"I know. Look, I'll explain everything, but do you mind if I shower first? I would love a good coffee too. It's been a rough couple of weeks."

His nerve shook her back to her senses. She narrowed her eyes at him.

"But of course. Milk and sugar with that?"

Her impromptu guest opposed a disarming smile to her sarcasm.

"Just milk, thank you. This way?"

"No, that's my bedroom. Stefan's is on the other side."

Nick's lopsided grin told her he already knew. Neve shot him the sternest glare she could muster. As if she hadn't enough of one alpha in her life. The confrontation was not going to be pretty.

*

She answered the door even before he had time to ring the bell.

"Hi."

His gaze travelled up to her face to meet hers. She was pale, her features marked in the dawning light. Her eyes were deep in their sockets, as dark and brilliant as polished amber.

"Where were you?"

"Boston. I had a meeting with the insurance company, and I stayed for the weekend."

"You should have told me."

"I told Terence."

"You should have told *me*," he repeated, leaning forward to brush her temple.

141

Her skin was cool, without a trace of a fever. She moved into his touch like a relenting cat, caving in the pleasure of his master's caress. Deep down, Ian guessed she hadn't called him for anything of the sort but he couldn't stop himself and cupped her face. Neve sighed softly, eyes fluttering closed. His free arm shot forward to bring her closer. She molded in his embrace. Anticipation ignited fireworks deep in the pit of his stomach. She reached up as Ian searched her face with darkening eyes.

A male voice cracked like a bombshell above their heads.

"Neve? Are you downstairs?"

Ian pushed her to arm's length.

"Who's that?"

Neve avoided his gaze, her delicate features downcast. He reached for his holster. She shook her head.

"It's not necessary…"

Above, the prowler insisted, "Do you want some coffee?"

Ian released his grasp on her shoulders. His face was stern once more, his gaze as hard as tarnished steel. Her heart sank a little too low for comfort. She tried to smile at him, to no avail, so she just forgot it and called out, "Make that two, will you? We have company!"

*

Ian frowned as he followed the man who claimed to be Nicholas Beneto's gaze. The Bureau implied Beneto was dead; a nameless body found in the park. Dead people didn't drink coffee on Sunday mornings while leering at comely women. He forced his hand to relax on his thigh.

"How do I know you're telling the truth? You're a crook or an assassin, most probably both; your word doesn't mean a thing."

142

"I guess you could call the FBI, but I'd rather you didn't."

"And why is that?"

For the first time, the easy smile vacillated.

"What do you think? *Cosa Nostra* ferreted me out in a federal safe house. They have a mole in."

"Who?"

Nicholas shrugged.

"No idea. I haven't seen much of anyone in the past three years. A couple of marshals; the prosecutor. A Tough cookie, that one."

"I should turn you in."

"Once again, I'd rather not."

"What about Stefan?"

Both men turned toward Neve. She folded the kitchen cloth to put it on the counter before her. Her hands were steady when he expected them to shake. Ian wished he knew what lay behind her question. Now was not the time for another one of her curveballs. Her amber-colored eyes slit on Nicholas.

"He's risking his life to finish what you've started. That's not fair."

Ian swallowed a smirk when the crook squirmed on his stool.

"I know. But there's nothing I can do about that."

"Yes, there is."

The blond detective shut up. He tried to read behind the calm demeanor, without success. Neve stared back at him, too serene for the coming argument. His blood flared and thickened in anticipation. She did enjoy make his life miserable.

Neve turned toward her guest with the same tranquil smile, "We won't be long."

Taking him to her bedroom didn't feel exactly comfortable, so she headed for the stairs. The wind had picked up outside, chillier than before. She buried her hands in her sleeves, blowing warm air on her knuckles through the knit fabric. Ian didn't allow her more than a second of rest before he barked.

"No."

Neve turned her back to the street to face him. "You don't even know what I'm going to ask."

"You want to put your lovely nose in something that goes well above your head; and mine. Messing with the feds, that's one step too close to felony. I could lose my badge. And you could get hurt, seriously hurt. We're talking about the Mafia here. Coppola got it wrong. There's nothing romantic about gangsters. Those people kill, Neve."

"Stefan's in danger."

Hesitation polished the stormy gaze fixed on her until it flashed like steel. She felt bad to call on his own code of honor. "If you hand Nicholas over, that man we found in the park would have died for nothing."

His retort drowned in the roar of an engine. Neve jerked her head toward the noise as the white truck sped down the street. Ian followed her stare just in time to see the window rolled down. He yelled, "Down!"

Her wrist twisted when she hit the sidewalk. Her cry of pain scattered in the backfire. Shards of glass pelted them as windows exploded. Something pinched on her cheek. She yelped and closed her eyes tight. The noise was deafening. She couldn't remember being more scared ever before. The rattle didn't relent. Eyes shut, she groped for Ian. Crouched behind her, he escaped her hands and pulled her further behind the car with one arm. Her heart jacked up her throat, pressure crushing her chest. Neve struggled to breathe.

"Stay down!"

More shooting fused above her head. Another gun boomed.

"Inside, quick!"

Like an automat, she obeyed the new voice, crawling along the four feet that separated her from the safety of her apartment. Gunshots burst through the air repeatedly. Tires screeched, and then nothing.

Chapter 17

For the second time in as many weeks, Ian found himself jingling with emergency response units, paramedics, and a smug Terence Whale. He relished the bustle. Barking orders was easier than facing the riot in the pit of his stomach.

Screenwriters had their characters gunning down culprits more often than they changed clothes. Real life was different. On a screen, you didn't bask in the reek of fear, sweat, and gunpowder. No TV shows displayed the nausea resulting from aiming at another being and pulling the trigger. Movie heroes were impersonal; they feel nothing. Feelings came after the queasiness, when adrenaline receded and the void required filling. Ian wished the pressure in his eardrums would lighten.

He avoided looking at Neve to concentrate on his debriefing, but his stare drifted back to her like a magnet. Her eyes were both hollow and too damn brilliant, the irises reduced to a shrunken golden band. The paramedic was cleaning the small cut on her cheek, her left wrist already bandaged. They'd been lucky. The car they used as a shield was not.

"Did you see who attacked you, Detective?"

Ian returned his attention to the officer in front of him. His mind automatically translated the question: 'Did you recognize them? What made you think you were in danger?' Instinct was just another way to describe a déjà vu impression. The body reacted first, brain catching up later.

"There were two men. I'm not sure if they wore balaclavas or not. Everything happened fast. The mini-van–"

Terence Whale barged in, "A Chevrolet express. White. Couldn't read the plates but it can't be hard to find. I lodged two rounds into the right wing."

Indifferent, the police officer scribbled in his notebook.

"And you are?"

"Terence Whale. Detective Braich here knows me. You're lucky I can still handle myself with a firearm, young man."

Ian pinched his lips but kept his mouth closed. The police officer wrinkled his nose. "So I assume you have a permit for that gun?"

The retort shut the older man up. Suspicion flashed on his face.

"I helped. Is that how you Americans reward good Samaritans nowadays?"

"No, Sir. But we are not accustomed to rehearsals of Buffalo Bill's Wild West featuring Great Britain citizens anymore. Are you the one who called 9-1-1?"

Ian bit back a grin at the deadpan. Whale shook his head, clearly upset by the lack of consideration for his gesture, or his age. He handed his .22 semi-automatic G&W with a snort, then turned tail with a grunt when reminded about his statement.

Probably Nicholas' doing, Ian thought. The crook was nowhere to be seen, which was just as well. The longer he stayed burrowed, the more time he'd have to see the bigger picture behind all this mess. Neve's assault, Nicholas' sudden reappearance, shooting in a quiet neighborhood, that was one coincidence too many.

"Will that be all, officer?"

"Yes, Sir. I need you to come to the precinct with me for a full debriefing. You'll have to wait two days before picking up your gun and return to your service. I'm sorry, Detective. You know—"

"The drill. Yeah, I do."

Ian balled his hand into a fist. Sorry or not, he was still out of the loop for the next forty-eight hours.

*

The man stood in front of the shelves, staring blankly at the scotch crystal bottle and his empty glass. He'd had only a glimpse; it'd been enough. He would recognize that face anywhere. He didn't give a damn about the girl, or her beau, but he could not afford them to pull on the right laces and untie the complicated web they were glued in.

He refilled the glass with two fingers of liquid fire and sipped it. Alcohol loosened the anxious knot in his back.

With his original plan in jeopardy, he needed to calculate his next steps carefully. Slip back in the shadows. Watch and wait for the right time to strike. After all, five million made a nice retirement egg too.

But first, he had some clean-up to do.

*

She assured the paramedic she was fine. She nodded when Ian come over to say he had to fill some form at the station. She smiled and dismissed him with a wave of her hand. All lies.

Neve tightened her grip around her burning-hot mug. She was not fine. She was scared and angry and hurt, and tired of being so. Her pulse throbbed against the too-tight bandage at her wrist. Her scalp, her shoulders, her legs, her whole body itched, on fire from adrenaline. She felt cold inside.

"Want some?"

Nicholas pushed a cookie bag toward her, Stefan's favorite brand.

"No thanks."

He selected one and munched at the roundness.

"You look like you could use a hug."

The proposal raised her hackles. Neve banged her hand on the counter. "In less than two weeks, I've been assaulted, harassed, and shot at, so keep your hands to yourself, and answer my questions!"

Nicholas swallowed the last of his biscuit and wiped the crumbles off his hands.

"I'm surprised you don't try to put the station's bombing on my back too."

"Don't tempt me."

He took one step closer to tower over her the same way Ian did when he wanted to physically impress her. Neve glowered. She wasn't taking the intimidation from the detective. No way was she going to give in to Nicholas.

The cutting glance failed to rebuff him. He leaned down and whispered against her cheek.

"Maybe you set your horses in too fast a gallop, Princess. Have you considered that you and your boyfriend were the only ones on that sidewalk?"

Her stomach lurched but she continued to scowl. After a second, he smiled.

"You're amazingly stubborn, you know that?"

Neve held the deep green stare without a word. Nicholas stepped back with a sigh. He walked toward a cupboard, pulling out two broad bowled wine glasses. "We're going to need more than herbal tea and cookies for that one."

*

Locks clicked open with a metallic echo. The man beamed, greedy hands coming forward.

"Hurry up, man. It's freaking cold in there."

Two pops, and he slumped on the floor. They had been warned: no more mistakes. He caught only one of them, but the other would get the message. The man unscrewed the silencer from his gun, glaring at the body. He put both items back in the suitcase and left the building without a second glance.

*

The staccato grew in intensity. The buzz that preceded it resumed; both vibrations made his back cry in pain. Ian pushed upright with a groan, the back of his throat parched. He snatched the cell phone from under a cushion.

"Neve? What's the matter?"

'Hello Ian... Who's Neve?'

Ian blinked in confusion.

"Mom?"

'Oh, honey... Did I wake you? You're generally still at the station at this hour...'

He tried to calculate the jet lag from South France. The math gave strange results and made his brain hurt.

"I'm on leave."

A cowardly way to put it but he wasn't in a hurry to tell his mother about the shooting.

'Leave? You? What happened? Are you all right?'

Concern peeked through the persistent fog that numbed his brain. He wasn't sure what questions he wanted to answer.

"I'm fine, Mom. It's been a long week..."

'Oh. Okay. So who's Neve?'

His mother wasn't one to forget a question, especially if it regarded a feminine presence in her son's life. Let the question of defining Neve.

Ian hesitated. The word 'partner' was going to fire more questions, 'friend' would be even worse. He could tell his mother Neve was just a witness in his current case, but he didn't want to reduce their relationship to that, if his mother even bought it.

He straightened up on the couch. The sports broadcast on TV was detailing the Olympic results of a men's downhill competition. Ian pinched the ridge of his nose between his thumb and index. Neve had lied to him about being fine. When had it started to matter?

A chuckle answered his silence.

'Fine, fine… You're off the hook for now. Just let me know if I need to add one plate for Thanksgiving dinner, all right?'

"Mom, we're in February. It's a little early to plan Thanksgiving."

'Feel free to bring her home sooner. I'm coming back in three weeks, so maybe Easter? We'll organize an Easter egg hunt for the kids, and-'

Ian cut in.

"How are they?"

Speaking about his sister's offspring was the best way to divert his mother's attention from her questioning. Annie had married some British hostel tycoon, and moved to Europe. When she had given birth to her fourth child, she had asked the happy grandmother to split her time between London or the Riviera depending on the season, and the East Coast.

'They're fine; we just came back from Monaco, which is why I'm calling so late, but we're returning this weekend. Ciaran...'

Ian let himself drown in the tale of his godson's exploits. After the last days' events, a weekend in the sun venturing in an aquarium with hyperactive kids felt like paradise.

"I wish I could come with you."

'I wish you could, too. I miss you. I'll call you when we come back to Bagnoles. Ian...'

She trailed off, not wanting to voice her worries out loud.

"I miss you too, Mom. Have fun!"

He hung up and leaned back in the couch. He was hungry, but the idea of fumbling with food was a bit overwhelming at the moment. Kermit prowled around his calves with an arched back and purred loudly, his feline way of demanding attention. He leaned forward to grab him but the cat zoomed out of reach toward the kitchen. Ian sighed, skidding closer to the edge to stand. Cats could be real pushovers.

*

"What do you know about the Families?"

Neve contemplated the rich red color in her glass.

"Not much. Several chapters split the pie between them. I know they're territorial, too."

"That's right. New England was always a battlefield between Irish mob and Italian *Cosa*. I'll spare you the history lesson, but what I can tell you is that the 1990 federal breakthrough only served to make it go underground."

"What happened in 1990?" Neve asked. She remembered an article last year about a major arrest in southwestern Connecticut. But those federal

152

investigations were so sensitive only a few details came out in the media.

"Since Spring 1990, several bosses of both sides were arrested all over New England. They were charged with racketeering, gambling, extortion, drug trafficking, murder, you name it."

"So they made peace?"

Nicholas shrugged.

"They had to if they wanted to escape the threat. Gambino kept the extortions and racketeering; the Winter Hill Gang took over thefts and drugs. They exchanged information about FBI moles and *delatori,* traitors."

"That's how you fit in that wonderful family picture."

Nicholas didn't answer the barb, lost in the contemplation of the label on the bottle. Neve watched him from under her lashes, hiding behind her glass, only half-ashamed for the unkind remark. It all started after Nicholas' disappeared from his safe house two weeks ago.

Her tired brain still spun to fit ill-matching pieces. Neve pouted in her wine.

"I hate being a human target."

"Trust me, sweetheart, so do I."

Her body started aching from head to toe, as alcohol allowed exhaustion to take over. All of a sudden, she felt very tired and close to tears.

"It's not going to end, is it? They won't stop until I'm…"

'Dead'. The last word inflated in her throat until it was too big to come out. Nicholas reached for her and this time she didn't resist the embrace.

Chapter 18

'The trial of the four alleged leaders of organized crime in New England is now back on track after Prosecution and Defense finally agreed on a choice of jury. Seven women and five men were retained. It won't surprise anyone to learn that none of them are of Italian or Irish origins. Defense attorneys were more discreet this time and allowed the process to run smoothly. It makes you wonder if the gunfight that took place three days ago on Harmon Street is a coincidence or not. The police and the FBI refused to comment. Of course, they are still sorting out the aftermath of the bombing at Central Station...'

Bourque tuned out the TV to face the detective perched on the edge of his seat on the other side of the desk. The tense expression on his face gave the whole scene an air of déjà vu.

"Lee called me about the van near the old butchery. I want in."

"Out of the question. You're too deeply involved. Let Peters and Yuan do their job."

"Of course I'm involved, the bastards tried to kill me."

The last remark grumbled low, more for his own benefit than his captain. Bourque leaned back in his chair. He stared at his man and the mute television in turn, then asked, "Are you sure?"

Ian stopped flexing his right hand and looked up. He opened his mouth to answer but no sound came out. After a full second, he shook his head. Bourque grabbed his phone from the receiver and waved his hand in dismissal.

"Then you don't have any reason to bug me. Carole, patch me through to–"

Ian stopped listening. He contemplated the brick wall behind the reporter on the screen a moment longer, and then walked out.

Deep down, he knew the bullets weren't for him. He silenced the inner voice that murmured about Nicholas. Nicholas Beneto was believed to be dead. If anyone had realized otherwise, he would never have made it that far.

For the hundredth time, the scene replayed in his mind. The van torpedoed down the street at the same time they'd walked out the door. They had to be already in the street, waiting, so the show wasn't for him either. The events cascaded along a too-obvious path leading to Neve. First, they tested her, then assaulted her at her office, and finally made a move, so she panicked and ran straight into a trap. But why? Why her? Why now?

The questions spun around in circles in his head, again and again. The answer was just a stone's throw away. He could feel it down to his gut. He missed a detail, a tiny, insignificant detail...

"Hey."

Ian glanced up from the keyboard in front of him. Sure enough, the unceremonious chirp came behind a mop of curly blonde hair.

"What are you doing here, Madeline?"

She crumpled her nose at the use of her first name. Ian glared back, uncaring if she didn't like the familiarity. After a full minute, the girl mumbled.

"Neve said that you'd want to talk to me."

He frowned. He hadn't heard from her in three days. He hadn't called, and neither had she. Instead, she sent her lost boy. Girl. Whatever. He barked, "About what?"

"How should I know? You're the cop. Ask me questions."

Her tawny eyes burned holes into his shirt. Ian blew out a breath, trying to control the irritation her smugness fueled inside him.

"I don't have time for that. You don't want to be here, so why don't you just tell me whatever Neve felt you had to tell me? Hmm? Spare us both the cat-and-mouse game."

She smirked at his choice of words. Ian backed in his chair, waiting. The eye contest lengthened on. Out of patience, he stood, grabbing her by the arm. Madeline hissed, "Take your filthy hands off me, or I shout rape."

This time it was Ian's turn to smirk.

"In the middle of my station? Sure it'll work..."

She bared her teeth, as if readying to bite. She was so stiff he could nearly hear her back scream in pain. The dark eyes gleamed with something he associated with fear. The tear on her sleeve looked new. She reminded him of the mouse caught in the cat's paws. Ian lightened his grip until his hands rested gently on the frail shoulders. Even that contact seemed too much for the girl, so he released her completely.

"I could do with some coffee, what about you?"

"I don't drink coffee."

"Stop annoying me. Come on."

A few minutes later, they were seated in a booth at the Bottom Stone, Ian with his coffee, his strange companion with a slice of pear and chocolate pie. He waited until she had forked most of her dessert into her mouth to ask, "So? What is it?"

The furtive look hit him again. What was it with females and their nasty habit of forcing him to tear word after word from them, as if they guarded the world's biggest secret?

Before he could complain, a small notebook appeared out of one of the pockets from her parka. Curious, he put his cup down and picked the book up. It was torn, covered with scribbling and tiny sketches. The sheets were dented and vaguely yellowed on the edges. Some lines were scratched in faded ink. Other forms were far more distinguishable.

Ian flipped through the pages. The details on the recent figures were amazing. He recognized dragons, stylized zodiac signs curling around elaborate alphabets.

"Those are great. Did you do it?"

Madeline shrugged but her fingers flew to her mug to her plate and fork, never settling in one place.

"Some. I like to draw."

Each page displayed a different drawing. Obviously she had used the notebook as a palimpsest, drawing above the previous sketches and scribbling. She'd even managed to integrate the more visible ones to her own designs.

Finally, he put the open notebook down on the table to look at his companion. Madeline was watching him expectantly. Ian chose his words carefully.

"Why are you showing me this, Madeline?"

The pale cheeks pinked slightly. Ian stared at the notebook next to his coffee. A piece of his puzzle fell into place.

"Neve doesn't know you're here, does she?"

She pinched her lips tighter, then she snatched the two loose sheets that were clipped against the back cover. She then laid them carefully side by side on the table above the open notebook.

*

Perplexed, Ian stared at the papers displayed in front of him. At first, he saw nothing more than the intricate illustrations. Now a study of the Town Father bronze statue stared at a cat sharpening its claws on a yellowish flower. He scrutinized the sketch. The sunflower became some crude, almost childish sun star. Beside it, something that could have looked like a fairy except its open mouth revealed razor sharp teeth. Madeline sighed impatiently and tapped the handle of her fork on the papers.

"Here. Are you blind?"

He neglected to answer the provocation and focused on the line she pointed out. Then he caught it. The line started from one page and continued on the other one. Ian grabbed the notebook and one page to look at them more closely. The pattern reproduced on the north-south direction. The lines were not completely straight, as if they had been drawn by hand on a bumpy surface. He narrowed his eyes, and noticed the numbers were all displayed close to the lines. Like marks. Going through the pages again, he noticed more lines, always crisscrossing in square angles, and more numbers.

Madeline stared at him with a triumphal grin. He asked, "What is it?"

Her face fell. "I thought you would know." She paused, inhaled sharply, and then blustered, "I–"

Her stare came across Ian's puzzled look and the teen snorted.

"Never mind. Should have known you wouldn't believe me. You're a cop after all. Your lot is all the same. Hand it over."

158

She tried to grab the papers back. Ian pulled them out of reach.

"Your opinion of me is awfully flattering, thank you. Now tell me why you decided to show this to me instead of Neve."

The scrawny girl nibbled at her lips. He ignored it to refocus on the girl squirming on her booth in front of him.

"I… I kinda took it from her office."

Ian frowned.

"You mean you stole it from her."

"No! It was a nasty day, okay? Neve told me to stay inside because the weather was so mean. I was bored and I wanted some papers to draw. She told me I could help myself with the office supplies. The notebook was in a box."

He tried to make sense of her babble.

"But you didn't tell Neve what you had found and kept it."

She shrugged again, scrubbing some imaginary dirt from the table with her nail. Ian signaled their waitress to refill their mugs. The girl asked, "Do you think it's important?"

He rubbed his chin out of habit, thinking. Some detail was out of place.

"When did you say you found this?"

"I didn't say."

He warned, "Madeline…"

"Fine! It was sometime last month… Don't know which day. We don't care much about watches and dates in the street, you know."

The quip fell into a deaf ear. Another piece clicked into place, the noise deafening.

"I have to go. I'll keep this."

"Hey! It's mine!"

Ian sneered.

"Crime evidence now, Sweetie. Try to keep your nose out of trouble, will you?"

"But–"

He stood, walking briskly to the cashier. Madeline cantered after him in the street.

"So I was right? It's important?"

"Maybe."

She grabbed her arm to make him stop.

"Come *on*! It's my discovery! I have the right to know!"

Ian heard some of Neve in the girl's imperious tone. It didn't make him smile. Madeline might be street-smart, she was clearly taking some of the beautiful PI's worse habits, for example the ones that added to his burden. Ian spun on his heels to face the teen. Standing, the top of her head barely reached his shoulders. She cringed when he took her by the shoulders. This time, he didn't let go, coercing her to meet his stare.

"I want you to go to a shelter. Or to Neve's. Tell her you want to stay for a couple of days." So the girl would chaperone her and Nicholas. If he was still there. "There's a guy with her, Nicholas. I want you to keep an eye on him for me."

"Jealous?" The girl smirked.

Jealous? No, he wasn't. But it annoyed him senseless that she hadn't called him first.

"Cautious. Now scoot. I have work to do."

Madeline jerked her head to the side. Ian had to fight not to shake some sense into her. Now that he knew where to look, he couldn't afford losing more time.

"I promise I'll get back to you as soon as I can."

Madeline muttered under her breath, "As if you cared."

"I'm not your normal cop. Now do as I say."

The blonde sulked, rubbed the heels of her boot on the sidewalk, and finally nodded. Ian released a breath he hadn't realized he was holding. The relief spreading in his chest made him ill at ease. He pushed the girl away with a grunt.

"Just stay out of trouble for a while, okay?"

She made a face, and started strolling in the opposite direction. He half-expected a finger to sprout out, but she just turned a corner and disappeared from his view.

Chapter 19

Neve shot a very annoyed look at the police vehicle parked across the street. The so-called protection followed her everywhere, from the gym to the grocery store. It made it impossible for Nicholas to leave the apartment, not to mention the constant reminder of *why* she needed the protection. Now she got it out of her system, she wanted to forget the bullets flying at her, the emptiness in Ian's stare, and the cold she felt inside.

"I still wonder if that's such a great idea."

Nicholas stepped in behind her, coffee mug in hand. She offered a dry smile to his reflection in the glass.

"It's not. But we're doing it nonetheless."

"*We* means you and me, and *I* am not overenthusiastic with *your* plan. What had Ian to say about it by the way?"

Neve overlooked the question and the tease under it returning her attention to the street below. She hadn't heard from the detective in four days. At first she needed the distance, and after she and Nicholas came to an agreement, she'd preferred not to have him around. If/when Ian caught whiffs of their plan, the storm promised to be epic. God knew Nicholas had tried to talk

162

her out of it, and he was more easy-going than the detective, by far.

She finally turned away from the window to find Nicholas staring at her with serious eyes.

"Are you ready?"

After a moment, she nodded. He grinned and the resemblance with Stefan's boyish beam was almost blinding.

"Let's put this show on the road, then."

She picked up her phone.

*

The only small coffee booth was the only one still opened as the day waned. While she waited for a cup, Neve eyed her red and blue tail circling the park at a snail's pace. The stone arches were as empty as they'd been the last time she came here. Her free hand closed around the cross of the Magnum in her pocket in an attempt not to play with the micro hidden by her collar. It was heavier than the Beretta Ian had chosen days ago, and somehow, the extra weight reassured her. Nicholas had texted her minutes ago that he was in place, safely arrived on site after her departure had drawn the police away.

From her position under the arcades, she could only guess his silhouette in the distance. Stefan's old wool hat pushed down hard on his head masked his forehead while a large green scarf came up to his mouth.

Even with a police patrol around and him in her office, her insides refused to settle. Coffee burned its way down to the pit of her stomach.

"Either you're very clever, or very naïve, Miss Lass."

She took her time to compose a neutral face before she turned. The man in front of her didn't wait for an answer.

"Where's Beneto?" she deflected the question.

"I know that you lied and I will prove it."

"I doubt that. Anyhow, the real question is *should you?*"

His coolness chilled her to the core. The man was too quiet, as if he had another ace up his sleeve. But she'd played enough poker to recognize the bluff. Neve sipped her coffee to buy herself a few more seconds, waiting for the tables to turn.

"I believe in the system, Agent Martin. I'm naïve like that."

The man in black raised his eyes to the passing police car, then smiled down at her.

"Why don't we take a walk?"

"I'm fine here."

"Ah, of course. Electronics. I assume you dragged your detective into this and that he is recording this conversation somewhere nearby? Civil gadgets have a rather limited range, at least when there's nothing to block them."

Neve forced herself to breathe and not look toward Nicholas while Martin plunged one hand in his inside pocket and showed her a miniature scrambler that looked like a pen.

"The perks of working for Uncle Sam."

She stood her ground. Martin sighed.

"Miss Lass, I've shown more patience than your interference actually deserves. So–"

Anxiety laced with anger and she hissed, "Patience? You tried to kill me! And Nicholas!"

Martin grabbed her arm. She jerked away but he tightened his grip. Neve resisted, to no avail. Her eyes darted toward the park. The police car was nowhere to be seen. Nicholas was too far away to help.

"Let me go!"

Neve pulled harder, working her way through those self-defense moves she was so proud of. Her elbow missed, so did her foot. No matter how hard she battled, he still dragged her away from the booth and the meager safety it provided. Fear buzzed in her veins, boosting her strength with panic. She yanked her arm to the side and reached forward in an attempt to grab the gun in her pocket. She was too slow. Martin's thumb pressed into the crevice of her forearm and she saw stars.

*

The blow took Ian by surprise. He fell on his knees, head first in the newspaper box. Skin broke, and blood gushed over his eye. Before he could react, another hit took him straight in the hip. He dodged before his aggressor could hit the same place again. Hurt exploded like firecrackers in his head, his side, his left knee. He reached for his holster, finding nothing. His firearm was still locked, waiting for some stupid clerk to sign him off.

Too many thoughts crossed his mind at the same time while he tried to stand. He wore his shield at the belt. The guy had to have seen his badge. He needed something to defend himself. The alley was so empty... The steel pipe swung again. Ian launched himself aside just in time to avoid a direct blow. The man knew he was a cop. He was taking a go nonetheless. The end of the pipe scraped his shoulder hard enough to send him down again. Ian spat blood on the sidewalk, tried to get up.

"You're... in for... trouble."

Nausea clogged his throat. Breathing became a scorching battle.

A part of him wanted to ball like a hedgehog and offer as small a target as he could. A black veil threatened to engulf him. Survival kicked in late. Ian rolled over his shoulder, grunted when pain shot up from it. He swerved and grabbed the pipe with one hand, its kinetic enough to help him upright. The world fluttered around him, darker around the edges. The pipe rose again.

He braced himself for the swing. If he could absorb the pain, make another run for the club...

*

"Ah shit... Damned devices never work when you need them," Nicholas seethed through his teeth. Another pang of static answered when he shook the tiny recorder close to his ear.

Half-rising from the bench, he squinted at the arcades but the large stone arches blocked his view. Neve was probably deep under the roof, protected from the wind. He hesitated to text her again. Every detail out of place could be deadly in the game she was playing.

"Come on..."

Neve's escort slowed in his peripheral vision so he stopped fidgeting to rest his back against the bench, his hands hidden from sight, as if he were just enjoying the winter late afternoon. The icy chill burned his lungs with every breath he took. The old man strolling the sidewalk to his right didn't seem to resent the cold, but he did. His guts kept nagging him about bad ideas and reckless females.

Once out of view of the blue and red, Nicholas hit the electronic device with his palm and shook it again. Another glimpse toward the arcades revealed nothing. The whole confrontation would be useless if he couldn't make this thing work. He gave her another five minutes before he rallied at her meeting point.

A familiar voice at his back startled him. "We need to get out of here. Neve baited the wrong fish."

Nicholas turned to meet his cousin. His motion for a hug stopped short when he saw the .22 semi-automatic in his hand. "Stef?"

"*Ciao*, Nick. Long time no see…"

*

A banshee howled. A flashing blur of yellow and gray blinded him.

Ian tottered backward, his heart jacking up his throat. The brute grunted in rage.

"*Focáil leat! Hoor!*"

Bent forward with one hand on his thigh, Ian fought the shadows channeling his vision. The spitfire on his attacker's back hissed and spat, both sounds all too familiar.

"Mouse! Don't! Go! Go away, now!"

Screaming ripped his chest apart. The man backed into the wall. Ian lunged into his legs, too late. Madeline slipped on the ground, motionless. Ian grasped the steel rod with both hands this time, banging it at random against the brick wall. The brute dropped his bludgeon. Ian dove for it.

The cold and blood made his hands slippery. He heard another nauseating noise, closer. The shriek drilled pain behind his right eye. Agony exploded in his head, like never before. White. Cold. And then nothing.

*

"Why are you doing this? You're serving the law…"

Neve stopped herself before she begged. She concentrated on her breathing, the sharp rasps coming out of her mouth thick with tears. Martin was dragging her in

167

the general direction of Nicholas' position. Hope flickered deep in her stomach. Micros might not work, but as soon as he saw her. She turned her head toward the bench in the snow, and found it empty. Nicholas hadn't stuck around. She'd been a fool to believe he wanted to do the right thing.

The world finally shuddered when a car stopped nearby.

"Sir, we may have a problem."

Neve's knees shook as realization dawned on her. No one was going to help her. Her police escort was a fake. Ian had been right about everything: about Nicholas, about her and her delusions. She should have stuck with insurance inquiries and lost person search. She'd wanted to do more, to be more than an obscure private investigator and failed, lamentably.

Martin released her arm but she stayed where she was, subdued. The men in front of her exchanged information in hushed voices. Her brain refused to make sense of their muttering.

'Take them in?'

'Yes, both of them! It's too late now for cover up.'

A shrill cut in. Martin's frown deepened by the second, scaring the butterflies in her stomach to death.

"What?... Call it in... I don't care!... His man, his problem!"

The hang-up finally snapped her out of her daze. Neve inched backward, readying to flee. The federal agent muttered, "Miss Lass. You and I still need to talk; about your license, among other things. I'll call you."

If she ever wondered what a deer caught in head lights might feel, now she knew. And she hated it.

Chapter 20

Ian snapped to consciousness, disoriented. The pounding in his head mimicked a severe case of hangover, so the constant sway in his back could be an aftermath. Taking in air felt like dragging fumes out of an empty dive bottle. He concentrated on breathing for a moment, too numb to move. His chest and shoulder weighed a ton. He licked his lips. They were hard as ice. His tongue tasted something else, metallic and crusty. Ian forced his lids to open. Pain drilled behind his left eye and he groaned. Instantly the wall behind him stopped reeling.

"Ian! Ian are you awake?"

"Madeline?"

Surprise coerced a fit of coughing that left him breathless. His trapezius muscles and biceps twisted into knots. He flexed his fingers the best he could. The skin of his wrists stung, like a Band-Aid you pull away too slowly, only a thousand times more painful. After a few seconds, he managed to fist his hands.

"We're cuffed."

"I noticed, Sherlock," Madeline hissed.

The spike in her voice sounded a bit like fear. Ian accepted the sarcasm. Sort of.

"Well, Houdini, can you do something about it?"

"I'm trying."

The hiccups and squirms in his back resumed. He gritted his teeth when her elbow grazed his hip. For a few moments, he heard nothing but groans and gasps. Ian tried to relax his arms to give her as much space as possible. He rolled his neck from side to side, fighting exhaustion. The place was pitch-black except an eerie rectangle about four feet high in front of them. A window maybe. He wondered how much time had passed.

"Where are we?"

"I don't know. I woke up here. Ah… Fuck!"

Metal screeched against metal. Madeline jolted in fury. The tugs flared the nerves in his arms to life. Pain, too.

"Huh, Madeline…"

"Sorry…"

This time, there was no mistaking the edge in her tremolos.

"It's fine. Try again."

Teeth clenched, Ian swallowed a curse when she pulled his wrists backward for more leverage. His shoulder strained so much he feared it would snap. The next second, Madeline mewled.

"Madeline? Madeline, talk to me."

The pressure in his back changed so quickly he nearly fell backward. Something hot and sticky wet his fingers.

"You're hurt?"

"I'm free," she seethed through her teeth. "Now what?"

Her question wobbled as if she was crying. Ian didn't push.

"Check my breast pocket, maybe the son-of-a-bitch didn't take my cell phone."

In the dark, Madeline floundered over his ribs to reach him. He wheezed when she touched a sensitive spot, but gulped the pain down. At least he could feel that. His legs, not so much.

"Nope, no phone."

"Okay, help me up, let's find out if there's a door attached to that spot over there."

He pushed up, struggling to stand up. With his hands still cuffed behind his back and his knees harder than concrete, he had to lay on the girl's small frame to straighten up. It surprised him when she kept her arms around his waist but said nothing, grateful for the help and warmth. He grimaced when blood started to flow down his limbs once more. His body started to remember the cold wasn't natural and the discovery was all but pleasant.

They tumbled to the door. Ian squinted at the grayish rectangle. It was a window of some sort, but even with his nose pressed to it, he couldn't see outside. Madeline let go of him to search the wall around it.

"I feel an edge, but there's no handle."

Her teeth hacked through the words so that panic could fill the gaps.

Ian rested his back against the door.

"Hey, we're going to find a way out of here, okay?"

He heard a snivel and guessed she'd shrugged. He forced conviction into his voice.

"If I'm not home for diner, Kermit will put on such a show the neighbors will figure out something's wrong anyway."

The comment was silly, and a long shot. But all children liked pets and if he could distract her for a while, maybe her desperation would not rub off on him. Not too fast anyway.

"Who's Kermit?"

"The cat."

"Too bad you don't have a hound dog; he would have picked up your scent despite the smell. It reeks in here."

Ian pushed himself up a bit, fighting to keep his eyes open. His shivers were receding again, pain ebbing away. Hurting was better than hypothermia.

"What did you say?"

"It reeks. Don't you smell it? It's worse than rotten food."

"Right."

It could be a coincidence. Tons of building in town could smell like decaying meat. Except he didn't believe in coincidences; never had.

"I think we are in or near the old butchery."

The exact place where they had located the van of Neve's attackers a couple of days earlier. His brain picked up from there. First a note, then shots, and a beat-up... He'd been warned, all right.

The Irish slang kept swirling around and around in his head. He'd heard the drawl before, yet he couldn't place it. Not that the knowledge helped with their current situation. Madeline snuggled closer in silence. Ian shifted to get comfortable with her added load on his ribs and his wrists caught between his lower back and the wall. Inhaling was the worst, like dragging in unsheathed blades on fire. He probably suffered a cracked rib; or two.

"We need to move. It's dangerous to sleep in the cold."

"Yeah, I know. Just give me a minute."

The black and white points that still flickered before his eyes spun madly, blowing out of proportion. The blast sent him crashing against the floor, and agony blinded him for good.

*

Nicholas turned the communications off.

"Books knows they are watched and taped. He isn't going to tell anything."

"Stefano might."

The young woman detached her eyes from the pair on the other side of the one-way glass to look at Martin.

"You knew! You knew that DA slug was your leak and you used me as bait, you son of a bit–"

"We had suspicions. Contrary to some people I won't name, the FBI does not throw accusations without proof," Martin sniggered.

"Go to hell."

The FBI agent sobered up, brows furrowed while he returned his attention to the interrogation room.

"Books played his cards so close to his chest we never saw it coming and I'm sorry for that. Jack was a good agent and a good friend. Your cousin said he hoped to gain a way out by giving you away. But why? If they had known about him, why come after you? You made a point in protecting your family before you got in. Books knew that. The Mafia doesn't do grand gestures anymore."

"You're saying that if they had known about Stefan Benedict, they would have come after him instead of attacking my safe house. That whoever blackmailed that little rascal is not *Cosa Nostra*."

"Yes, exactly."

"Then I understand even less the game you're at here."

Martin didn't answer, and switched the speakers on again to listen. Nicholas took his cue and shut up, wondering how Neve was going to take the news...

Chapter 21

The ring startled Kermit who abandoned his vigil at
the foot of the counter and the glazed ham cooling on the
plate for safer ground behind the couch. Ian grouched and
had to wait a few seconds for the world to stop waltzing
before he dragged his feet toward the door. The intruder
was in for a big, fat, well-deserved piece of his mind.
He'd had a shitty day, hell, a damned shitty week, so
whoever was hanging onto the screeching bell better have
a hard, concrete reason to bug him.

"Hi. Lauren gave me your address…"

Neve's mild smile quivered. She stepped forward as
if to hug him but Ian kept staring. Her arms fell back to
her sides. She hadn't been sure about coming. If his
reaction was any indication of Ian's mood, maybe she
shouldn't have.

He grumbled under his breath, too low for Neve to
be sure if he was inviting her in or not. She chose the
former and Ian retreated deeper inside the apartment. Her
stare wandered around, taking in the lit large flat screen
and comfortable couch, before it stopped on the man in
the kitchen. She gulped when he pushed the sleeves of his

176

jumper up, revealing a large bruise on one wrist and bandages around the other.

"You look…" Neve struggled, looking for a better word than 'terrible,' "…rough."

He threw her a glance over the counter.

"That's what two cracked ribs do to a man. What do you want?"

"Why are you so hostile?"

"I'm not. I'm tired, I'm hungry, and every single part of my body is hurting so you'll excuse me if I'm not into small talk right now."

He turned away. Irritation craned its way up her spine. Why did he always have to make things so difficult? She thought they had finally reached some kind of equilibrium after… Neve jostled when she felt fur wrap itself against her ankle. Looking down, she noticed the ginger and cream cat looking up at her.

"Hey you…"

She crouched and petted the soft back. Satisfied, Kermit purred and allowed her to pick him up. Ian concentrated on the pot that exuded whiffs of herbs and melted butter. Neve walked to stand beside him, Kermit comfortably settled on her forearm with his front paws on her shoulder, his nose buried in her hair.

"Ian…"

He dropped his spoon in the casserole to whisk the cat from her arms and put him back on the floor. The gesture was completely childish and annoying, and she would have resented it if his breathing when he straightened up hadn't turned into a heart-wrenching wheeze.

"Why are you here, Neve?"

She brushed his shoulder, hating herself when he winced.

"Why don't you go lie down while I finish this?"

She pointed at the sauce simmering on the stove.

"I'm good."

"Ian, don't make me hit you."

His mouth curled on one side, the ghost of that irritating smile of his she never thought she would miss.

"Wouldn't you love it."

Neve overlooked the barb to examine a small vial on the counter, then turned her attention back to the meal.

"Do you have a potato ricer?"

"The third drawer from the top, on your left…"

He turned slowly but she stopped him.

"I'll get it."

Overpowered, Ian retreated to the couch grouching about being chased from his own kitchen. After a moment, the voice of the news anchor filled the room.

Ian scratched Kermit's chin while the cat nestled on the back of the furniture. Neve mashed the potatoes, smiling when the cat stretched his back legs in contentment with that special face only satisfied cats made. She searched the cupboard and drawers for plates, glasses and cutlery then quickly set the table.

"Boys! Dinner's ready!"

Kermit's head snapped up. Ian stretched with a wince, but scrambled up to his feet. Neve stepped forward as he rose, a bit wary because of the way he nursed his right arm close to his chest.

"You–"

"Thanks for dinner, Neve."

She'd be damned if she pretended she didn't like the kiss he landed on her cheek.

Halfway through the meal, Neve decided that she had heard enough about the weather, the Olympics, and the upcoming Academy Awards.

"Are you going to tell me who used you as a punching bag?"

So maybe the question wasn't her best try at diplomacy, but he wasn't a champion of euphemism himself either.

"I'd rather not talk about it."

Neve pushed her plate away.

"Do you want to talk about Madeline, then?"

Ian glanced up with half a smirk on his lips.

"I was wondering when you would ask about that."

"Well, we both know she's not a super fan of cops, and how she reacted to you the other night, so…"

She trailed off, chewing on her cheek while her face warmed up. Ian drained his glass before he refilled them both. Did those painkillers make his throat dry?

"What did she tell you?"

"Seriously? *'Nothing to talk about'.*"

"Smart girl."

Neve narrowed her tawny eyes on him, her glare stating '*You're exasperating*' even better than her mouth would have. Ian chuckled and regretted it instantly, each cough tearing bits of his chest apart. Neve reacted at once.

"Couch? Or bed?"

He glared in silence, hunched with his fists bone white as he struggled for a breath. She stood.

"Couch, then."

He delayed, half dreading the effort, half curious to see how she would react. Neve stepped closer, slipping one hand over his shoulder to steer him to the living room.

"Wicked little me adores seeing you in pain, and I'm here just to be able to relish your misery. Move."

Her quirked brow made him obey. Resting his back against the cushion she'd fluffed felt like Heaven. Kermit licked his chops in appreciation of her Florence Nightingale's tendencies then jumped from his perch on

179

the back of the couch to trot toward the kitchen when she returned to the sink with their plates.

"Don't let him fool you, he already ate."

The indignant snort that followed confirmed the feline had hoped for a little extra.

Ian focused on the local news, his breathing as shallow as possible so the feeling of being stabbed every few seconds became bearable.

"Huh, Neve, I think you should see this."

"What?"

"Isn't that… Stefan?"

To his surprise, she sighed and returned the glance with a flush.

"Yes… Yes, that's him."

Ian helped himself up with his fists.

"Is there anything you forgot to tell me?"

She sat on the opposite side of the couch, his stern expression enough to fire her up.

"And is there anything you avoided telling me about Madeline's being trapped with you in a cold room?"

"I was getting there."

"So was I".

"Ladies first."

"Ian, you're acting like a child!"

He flashed a boyish grin with the last word meant to disarm her.

"Ditto."

Neve rolled her eyes.

"You're impossible."

Lip balm gloss made her mouth shimmer like freshly washed fruit. For a moment, Ian considered tugging her close to end the argument with a kiss. His body felt stiff and heavy. She was soft and warm, a willing cure to his pain, so his brain took a minute to register why instead of feeling her curled against his side, she said, "I made a big mistake."

*

The door cracked open. A sharp pincer took care of the alarm system. One look at his watch announced he had about twenty minutes before the central command put its missing signal program into gear. He couldn't afford more than that. Anyhow, now the cat was out of the bag. Who knew what the little rascal was telling the police after their roller-coaster ride around the Arcades.

The burglar switched on the torch he brought with him. The discreet bloom swept along the kitchen and the two alcoves he guessed led toward bedrooms. He'd start there. Closet or nightstands were a good place to keep family mementos. He circled what looked like an old army rucksack.

A gurgle froze him with one gloved hand on the door. He backed away a few steps, just in case ears were straining. These old buildings always creaked and squeaked. But the waterfall echoed loud and clear; too close. There was someone else in the apartment. The girl. It ought to be the blonde girl who came in earlier. He'd seen her before at the office, lurking around on the pretense of informing Neve. He'd assumed she had left. She usually came and went like a leaf on the breeze.

No need to glimpse at the clock to know he had less than eighteen minutes now. Time was running thin, as were his options. He had no choice. Terence Whale clicked off the heavy Maglite.

*

The TV shut off with a dingle. Ian held the remote a second longer before he put it down on the sofa between them.

"Aren't you going to say something?"

181

"Say what? Neve, you accused a federal agent of corruption, without proof, while your assistant–"

"Former assistant. I–"

He glared at the interruption. Disappointment sharpened the ice in his voice to an edge.

"Your *roommate* threatened to hand his own cousin to the Mafia with the gun I lent *you*, no less!"

Neve pinched her lips; she stared at him with shiny eyes for a moment then stood. She was already picking her coat off the hook when she heard her name come out strangled.

"Neve…"

His hand on hers over the knob stilled her. How had he managed the stealth in his condition, she didn't know. Neve took air in before she forced a gentle curve on her lips and turned.

"I… have early phone calls; tomorrow. I'll go now."

He pressed his forehead to her, bringing her close. The ghost of fever on his skin reduced her defenses to rubble.

"You're mad at yourself more than me."

"That's not a reason to rub it in. I might lose my license; my whole business…"

Her voice quivered so she shut up. He was right. She was furious with herself for making such a rookie mistake, the hasty judgment without solid proof. She was anxious, and disappointed with his reaction. Or was she? She'd asked for it; maybe she was hoping that hearing it out loud would help. It didn't. Ian sensed the despair swelling inside her stomach, and embraced her tighter. She rested her head in the crook of his shoulder, returning the embrace. They stayed like that for a moment, until her brain caught up with his labored breathing.

"You're okay?"

"Hmm… Quite comfortable actually…"

The painkiller had finally kicked in and slurred his words slightly. Neve extricated one of her hands from between them with the intention to untangle his from the small of her back. He shifted just enough to block her. His chin rested on her hair. She changed her tactic.

"You're heavy, Ian…"

"Weren't complaining 'bout it the other night…"

Her face fired up. She smacked his forearm slightly.

"Ow…"

"Yes 'ow'. Let me go, my phone is chirping."

As if on cue, the small whistle echoed again, to Kermit's great interest. Ian consented to lift one arm so she could slip under his elbow and reach her pocket.

What she heard on the phone drained her face of color.

Chapter 22

"He's going to hurt Madeline! Please, let me go, I have to–"

Ian tugged at her wrists.

"Neve, they're gone. If anything, you're going to tamper with evidence. You stay here. I'll handle it."

Neve shook her head, thrashing to break free.

"You must trust me on this. What did he say?"

"Something about the *Sea of Galilee*."

The sing-song drawl had been familiar, the words foreign. If only she knew what he meant… Madeline… She should never have let her alone; it was her fault, her fault again if someone got hurt... Her head spun faster with each heartbeat, so hard it hurt to keep her eyes open. The pressure between her eyebrows increased. The world gloomed and slowed down, and she finally managed to take in air.

Ian brushed his thumb against her forehead one more time before he released her. Her lashes fluttered open. He winked.

"Ex-girlfriend was into alternative medicine; Chinese pressure points or something… What's the *Sea of Galilee*?"

She was grateful for his to-the-point questioning, disquieted by her panic attack. Neve tried to collect her thoughts before she answered.

"I don't know! I don't know what it is… Ian…"

Her pulse spiked once more; her fists were so clenched they trembled. Neve concentrated on counting up to four while she blew air in and out, like an apnea diver before he plunges underwater. Ian grabbed the phone on the table near the door.

"Luke? Ian… Good enough. Look, is Lauren with you? I need you to do me a favor… Listen carefully."

He stepped inside his bedroom and Neve stopped listening. Ian was right, she wasn't thinking straight. She had to calm herself, to look at the prospects with a detached eye. Whoever had abducted Madeline knew her and her relation with the girl. He knew where she lived, and managed to observe her undetected in the past few days. So it was someone she was acquainted with, and never saw as a threat. Neve let out a sour snort. Up until a few hours ago, she believed her roommate was a clumsy merry-andrew without a mean bone in his body. Her judgment of people could use some sharpening.

Peering around, she noticed the small desk with his computer. She needed only three clicks to open Google, and load her request.

Neve scrolled down the page, certain geography and biblical references were not what she was looking for. The sting on the back of her constricted throat announced bile was rising up again. She clicked on Images out of despair.

"Oh God… Ian, that painting…"

Rembrandt's only known seascape filled the screen.

"What about it?"

"That's what he wants, the *Storm on the Sea of Galilee*."

Ian leaned over her shoulder and typed a new search. She paled when she read out loud the next page that appeared.

"The stolen artworks included several painting by Rembrandt, the most famous being the *Storm on the Sea of Galilee*, Vermeer's *Concert*, several Degas' drawings, a Manet's and bronze pieces."

She swallowed. How could she find pieces of art lost to the world for twenty-four years? Ian pointed at the forest of crosses that created the illusion of masts on the screen and his words rendered her speechless for good.

"I've seen this before."

*

Ian watched the beautiful PI as she busied herself with the wireless kettle. She insisted on making a fresh teapot, though he had a feeling bourbon would do a lot better for their nerves than Earl Grey. He pondered his second call, and Neve's reaction when she would find out. Happy and thankful came far up on the list. He sighed. Ripping Band-Aids off was always easier.

"I called Martin."

The kettle touched base with a clang and she turned, her gaze unfocused for less than a second.

"You what?"

"The Isabella Gardner heist is FBI jurisdiction. We need him. I did what I had to do and if you wer–"

Her reply hitched an octave higher than normal.

"Of course you did… You can't do wrong, after all. You're the perfect detective, when I'm just an idiotic amateur."

"Neve…"

"You just signed Mouse's death warrant!"

He held her furious glare, the need to justify himself already raging to step out.

"Sorry to interrupt, the door was opened…"

Neve broke the eye contact just long enough to shoot an equally murderous scowl at Nicholas.

"What are you doing here?"

She blinked twice, waiting for her brain to stop screaming outrage at Ian and connect the dots. Meanwhile, Ian plucked the tin can that contained his favorite Assam brand off her hands.

"Martin sent him, I assume."

He nailed the cap back on the box with more force than necessary after filling the pot. If she hadn't known better, she would have sworn he was sulking.

"You requested information on the 1990 art theft. So, how can I be of service?" Nicholas insisted with a lopsided grin, visibly enjoying the attention.

Ian snarled, "Quit the act, I'm not in the mood. What do you know about the heist? Were you involved?"

"Not I. Neve's brother."

*

"Mark was good with people. He blended in. Five minutes in a hostile crowd, and one half would swear they knew him for years while the other patted him on the back. That particular talent made him very useful for scouting. He would go in and gather whatever intel the team wanted, sweet as pie."

Nicholas slipped an apologetic smile Neve's way. She didn't return it, her lips pressed together firmly. Ian asked, "And the Isabelle Gardner?"

"It was no exception. Mark befriended some guys from his art class, and somehow convinced them to hold a Christmas party at the museum where their roommate worked at night. So he learned it all. The guards' names and habits, their routine, the alarm system, everything. Mark relayed the information and they made the coup on St. Patrick's morrow."

Ian glared.

"How do you know all that?"

"I drove the van."

"So you know where the pieces of art are?" Neve whispered. Her pale cheeks and the strained look on her face suggested she had mustered all her strength to speak. Nicholas shook his head.

"No. We separated in a warehouse near the butcher district."

Ian winced in recognition but stayed quiet, letting the other man go on with his tale.

"Mark was in charge of keeping the loot out of sight until we could smuggle it away."

"And then the shit hit the fan," Ian interrupted.

"How so?" Neve asked.

Nicholas answered for him.

"The FBI was set on eradicating the vermin, once and for all, Italians and Paddies alike. Our *padrone* got caught in the cross-fire. Those who refused to switch allegiances went underground. Mark feared for your safety, so he decided to take the best offer he had."

"My father."

Nicholas nodded at Ian then gulped down the last of his tea. The detective stifled a grunt as he twisted on his stool for a more comfortable position. The drug induced numbness had already worn off thanks to the rush of adrenaline. Neve emerged first from under the avalanche of information.

"Where does all that leave us?"

"Hello, everyone."

Three pairs of eyes turned toward the door and the couple standing there. Ian narrowed his eyes on the newcomers and groaned.

"Great, now it's a party."

"The door was opened."

Luke smirked at his partner while his sister proceeded to bolt said door, a thick leather portfolio squeezed under one arm.

"So I've been told," growled the detective under his breath. Neve shushed him and stepped forward to help their friends out of their coats, which had him wonder when she had started acting like the lady of the house. Not that he minded, but Luke's amused expression annoyed him. Lauren ignored his grouch and went to the kitchen to greet Nicholas. Luke lowered himself to the sofa with a groan of relief. Ian hesitated then imitated him.

"How's the leg?"

"Stiff. How're the ribs?"

"It only hurts when I breathe."

They exchanged a look then hunched over the small camera Luke had extracted from his sister's portfolio. The rest of the group ended their kitchen party to join them.

"The lock had been picked. The apartment was empty."

Lauren flipped through the pictures, passing the camera around once in a while.

"I found a towel on the floor in the bathroom, but the tub was dry. With the portable heater on, I can't say how long they were gone."

"Mouse was still soaking when I left around 6 p.m.," Neve said. Ian checked his watch out of habit. The short hand was yet to reach the last quadrant "and I received the call at 8:13 p.m."

"At least one hour then; maybe two."

"Blood?"

Ian closed his eyes not to see distress paint over Neve's face once more and concentrated on Lauren's report.

"No. No traces of a fight, either. They must have taken her by surprise."

"They could be anywhere."

He couldn't escape the lilt of panic in her voice. Ian watched as Lauren hunched over her portfolio once more. Knowing what she was looking for, he backed into the sofa.

"It wasn't easy to scan it properly without dismembering it, but Caleb did quite a job with the notebook, starting with those scribblings–"

"What scribblings? What notebook?"

Lauren slid Ian a glance that said 'Your mess, not mine' while Neve marched toward them. He complied as fast as he could, and braced himself for the explosion.

"Madeline came to see me a couple of days ago. She wanted to give me this." He pointed at the notebook on Lauren's lap. "She found it under your desk or something. I asked Lauren and Caleb to have a look because of a series of lines and numbers we couldn't decipher."

"Was that before or after you were banged up?"

She'd added two and two faster than he had.

"Before. They can't have known, Neve, I went directly to the lab, and Mouse certainly didn't talk about it to anyone."

She brushed the argument aside, one hand flipping in the air like a tennis backhand which made him glad he was seated by her side, after all.

"And you are only telling me about it now?"

"Hey, I was beaten into a pulp right after that. Besides, there was no point! How could we relate it to anything without a proper–"

"The *point* is that this notebook is *mine*! A roll in the sheets doesn't give you the right to mess through my belongings as you please! You and your *manic* urge to control everything! It's your fault if my friend was kidnapped!"

"Rather her than you."

The comment shut her up more efficiently than any retort, though her eyes continued to scream. Ian held her stare without blinking. Time froze while they challenged each other until Nicholas cleared his throat.

"Huh, I was under the impression the clock is ticking."

"I wouldn't start if I were you," Neve said dryly. "You knew, all this time; you knew someone was after me, and about my brother, you knew everything and you never said a word. I need some air." Her voice shook and died in a blizzard.

Two minutes on the small balcony coated the angry squirrels in her head in ice, so they slowed their spinning to a more reasonable pace. The door cringed behind her and cautious hands put her coat on her shoulders and withdrew, as if Lauren wasn't sure she would allow the contact. Neve pulled it tighter around her, her lungs burning from the icy air.

"If you're about to say he was just protecting me, save it."

"He probably thought he was, but the truth is he sucks at team work."

She met the technician's eyes. "Luke can rattle on about it for hours."

"He sucks at apologizing, as well."

"You have no idea."

Neve glanced through the half-fogged window at the three men in the room. Ian lifted his head to glimpse their

191

way, his face guarded. She looked away. Lauren shivered.

"Look, you have every right to be mad, but he's a good cop. We have a better chance of finding that girl with his help. You'll make him sweat for it later. I'll help."

"This is the best argument I've heard all night."

A new spark ignited the amber eyes. Lauren nodded in satisfaction.

"So you and…"

"I'm not sharing details."

"Can't blame a girl for trying. Come on, we have work to do."

Chapter 23

The caretaker closed the door of the room with a sigh. The girl weighed less than a hundred pounds, but taking her out of the apartment to the next building had been taxing. He was getting too old for this. That brunette earlier had never caught him on his way out. At his age, it was easier to hire hands for the dirty jobs; like Shane, who'd given a fair warning to that cop.

He worked the kink at his elbow while retreating to the living room. The girl was tied up and gagged, so no one would hear her wake up. He would have preferred to bring her to the storage upstairs, but his spare room would do for now. He cleared his throat, annoyed. He should dust that room more often. His mouth felt parched. He shrugged. Nothing a good swig of brandy wouldn't cure. Unless he indulged in an Irish coffee? He needed to stay awake.

Terence Whale snorted. Cops all stunk, female or not. He would keep watch tonight. And call Shane to get rid of the girl.

*

Neve frowned at the flakes that dusted her windshield. The snow was clogging her wipers, despite or because of the windshield washer fluid. At least the messy streets forced her to push questions and doubts to the back of her mind so she could concentrate on driving.

She ignored her passenger's muffled grumble and squinted at the drifts that bordered the glittering patch of asphalt. The turn was there somewhere. White upon glistering black glared back at her. Her hands weighed too much on the wheel and the car drifted to the left.

Ian groaned as he bent to retrieve his pistol. She huffed.

"If you put that away in its holster–"

"I can't."

She gritted her teeth loud enough for him to hear.

"I can't wear the straps with the bandages."

Neve suddenly noticed how his fingers hooked in the safety belt to keep it from tightening around his ribcage. His bandaged ribcage; with cracked ribs. She'd forgotten he was hurt. Guilt lumped up in her throat. Unable to swallow it back, she clenched her fingers on the wheel and focused on the road. Silence thickened the air between them again.

She hadn't asked him to come. He could be hanging on his phone trying to light a fire under God knows who, or sleeping, for all she cared. She was angry at him. She had every right to be. He kept things from her, papers that belonged to *her*, even after she shared her secrets with him. She should have known better than that. Less than two weeks ago, she was wary of the very air he was breathing, and it should have stayed that way. Because of him…

The clutch jammed, followed by an alarming *vroom*. Ian leaned forward. For a second, she thought he was aiming at the steering arm. Neve fisted it tight. Blue eyes burned a trail along her jaw. She barked, "What?"

He braced himself on the dash to turn fully toward her.

"God, you're stubborn. Just release that pedal, press again and then shift."

She fought to change gear.

"Damn it, Neve, can't you accept help when it's offered?"

Suddenly, the opening she was looking for jumped in front of her. Neve jolted and pulled at the wheel to turn. Without the motor restrained, the tires spun on a patch of frost. The brakes refused to respond. She pressed the pedal harder. Her pulse mimicked the staccato of packed snow on the discs. The back of the car swerved, irresistibly pulling in the wrong direction. She swallowed hard and let go.

The car skirted on the snow for an eternity, then bumped softly into a snowbank that was a mailbox, once upon a time. Ian's shield and sidearm slipped from his lap once more. She glared at them, deafened by the rush of blood in her ears. Her lungs burned from the breath she still held.

"You okay?"

"Fine."

"Neve..."

"I'm not talking to you."

"Good, so then you can listen."

Neve pressed the now free clutch. Before she could switch gears, Ian stole the keys from the ignition.

"I'm serious, you listen to me."

"Give me my keys back."

"In a minute. You're angry because you're panicked, and neither is going to help Madeline. Right now I'm the only one calm enough to actually *think*. You're rushing forward without the slightest idea of where you're going; which–"

"I'm going home."

Ian continued without acknowledging the interruption, "Which is exactly why I didn't tell you about Madeline's discovery right from the start. You need to calm down, now."

He paused, maybe waiting for a retort. No way in hell was she going to allow him the pleasure of one. She pinched her lips to a thin line.

"Trust me, I don't want to say this, but you have to accept that our chances of finding art pieces lost for more than twenty years are slim."

"I'm not listening to this."

She gripped his lapels with one hand, the other aiming at the keys.

"I'm not done."

Her hands balled into fists.

"I'll hurt you if I have to."

"So you keep saying. If it helps clear your head, be my guest."

She recognized the bait a mile away. He riled her on purpose, so she lost her temper and drove his point home for him. But damn him if she wasn't *tempted.* The breath she exhaled fogged the windshield further. Her fingers clutched to his lapel hurt. She released him.

"I need my keys to put the heater back on."

"No more driving into snowbanks, all right?"

Neve glared at the jab. Ian dropped the keys in her palm, closing her hand over it. She wrenched away from his touch without consideration for the cloud that dimmed his features for a breath.

*

He surveyed the corridor while she disarmed the system. Ian couldn't help but think they had failed to see what was right under their nose. And that irritated him more than the sulking woman by his side. No matter, he preferred that she resented him rather than chasing a wild goose in her tow.

"Who knows about your relation with Madeline?"

"Stefan; the people at the refuge; dozens of people, really…"

"No, not dozens of people. We are looking for someone who knows you care for the girl, who knew your brother's past, and who has access to this place."

"It can be anyone, Ian! Anyone could have seen me with her, and report it to the right person! I just–" she inhaled sharply to regain control of her emotions. "Whatever. I suppose Madeline found the notebook in my desk?"

She proceeded to the furniture without waiting, not even bothering to switch the lights on. Ian leaned a shoulder on the window frame with a grimace. The back alley below was empty, save for a beige Toyota Camry rolling backward toward the building. He pitied the poor guy who had a delivery in this weather. Ice trimmed the interior pane of the window.

Neve muttered, "I need some light here."

"Wait." Ian stepped sideways from the frame, brows furrowed as he squinted at the silhouette who had stepped out of the car.

"What?"

"This guy… Stay here!"

He hadn't had a good view of the man, but the military army cap was enough to identify him.

"Ian!"

Neve yelled after him, but he was already halfway down the stairs. He yelled back, "Close the door!" before he rushed out. A twinge of pain teased his chest with ice and fire. Ian groaned, stopping for a millisecond. So running with cracked ribs wasn't the best idea. He reached in his back for his Glock. Fuck that. The bastard owed him one.

A hand on his shoulder made him jump.

"What are you doing?"

"I just saw an old friend. I'll be right back. Go back up."

"I love friendly reunions," she said, narrowing knowing eyes on the arm he kept behind him.

Ian gave her a cheeky smile.

"Maybe next time, honey. See, Big foot and I, we have some kind of history between us, and I don't want you to see that side of me so early in our relationship. I'll meet you in your office, okay?"

Ian kissed the top of her head while she stared at him with her mouth agape and escaped through the front door.

Neve looked at the closing door, and wondered if she was shocked, awed, or very worried. She settled for a little bit of each, though the very last notion sent disagreeable shivers along her spine. It didn't take Sherlock Holmes' brain to understand he was going after an old foe. Was it linked to Madeline's kidnapping? Then who? Amusement left place to irritation as she realized that Ian had left her behind one more time.

Turning away from the stairs, she grabbed the knob, ready to yank the door open.

"Miss Lass; fancy meeting you here."

*

Ian winced with each step that made the snow crunch under his feet. The brick wall covered his approach, but he made too much noise, he could kiss the surprise effect good bye. Considering how strenuous breathing was, he labored no illusion of his chances if he lost that little advantage. He glimpsed in the alley; the brute was bent toward his trunk, and paid no attention to the surroundings.

Ian cocked his gun under his coat to muffle the noise and shifted as quickly as he could.

"Police! Kneel with your hands over your head!"

Unfortunately, he wasn't quick or silent enough. The muzzle of a firearm flashed. The shot ran over his head. Ian flattened against the wall. Another bullet shot too close on his left. The detective waited for the next round. None came. The car door banged. He stepped forward and opened fire as the motor roared. A window shattered. Ian took cover again. He was protected for now, but if the car exited the alley…

Silencing the ache in his side when he took a centering breath, he circled the corner and emptied his clip on the moving car, first at the now broken windshield, then the tires.

Ian stepped aside to reload at the same time the horn started blaring. Holding his gun at eye level, he crabbed his way toward the motionless car. His body cast a shadow on the hood. As if sensing the danger, he ducked. A third projectile ran loose. Ian shot three times at the driver.

Down on his haunches, Ian waited. A full minute passed, and nothing. Still bent, he circled the car from behind carefully, he slowly opened the passenger door. Big Foot was slouched back in the seat, his face bloody, a sawed-off shotgun angled down. He was still breathing. Ian snatched the gun from between his legs and threw it a foot away.

Hissing curses through his teeth, he looked for something to tie the man, while fishing his cell phone from his back pocket.

"I need an ambulance and a street car on Harmon," he looked at the door number, "1021. Gun shot. The suspect is alive, but unconscious. Yes. Number's 7554219."

"I truly wish you hadn't placed that call, Detective Braich."

Ian spun on his heels. Neve's amber eyes pleaded him to act. The gun pressed on her temple suggested otherwise. He growled, "You."

"Me. I suppose that ambulance is for Shane here. Ah well; since I can't rely on him anymore, I fear you'll have to do the dirty job in his place."

Terence Whale motioned him to put his gun on the ground. Ian didn't budge. The old man frowned.

"Don't test my patience, Ian."

The short hair on his neck bristled, but he couldn't do anything without Neve getting hurt. Ian gritted his teeth. He tossed his Glock in the snow and held his hands up, palms opened. His ribs protested. He doubled over, winded by the agony.

"Help him get inside. Now."

Chapter 24

"Pacing like this is not helping with your leg, and it's certainly not helping me concentrate. Can you please sit down?"

"His phone's disconnected."

Luke ignored the barely disguised order to frown at the receiver.

Lauren glanced up from her microscope.

"So?"

"So why did Ian cut off his cell phone? We agreed that we'll call as soon as you have more information."

"Which I don't."

"Doesn't explain why I can't reach him."

"Have you tried Neve's?"

Lauren gave her brother a pointed look.

"That's what I thought. Do that, and let me work."

*

The frustration in Ian's eyes was nearly enough to glaze over the pain, Neve decided, but not completely. Whale picked his cell phone out and dismantled it, pocketing the battery while tossing the case away. His groan trembled close to her ear, as she put his arm around her waist and helped him inside.

"Are you all right?"

"Better than it looks."

His whisper puzzled her and she gawped. Ian pressed his palm on her hip even so he leaned into her. She paused, worry painted over her face. For a fake, the cold sweat on his forehead was very realistic. Ian squeezed her waist again. She took in air, and prayed she'd read him correctly.

"Terence..."

Pleading tore her throat apart. Besides, the caretaker knew her as a strong, independent woman. Neve hardened her voice.

"Ian is wounded. He has to at least sit down."

SaidIan tensed subtly, moving between her and the other man. Whale waved at the couch with his pistol.

"Where's Madeline?" Ian asked, while Neve piloted him through the room. Once again, he sounded wheezy while his legs were steadier than they should and she wondered if she'd missed something.

"Ah, the good old cliché: the hero tries to make the villain reveal all his plans. The plan is fairly easy. Miss Neve here has twelve hours to find the loot. After that, she'll decide which one is to die first, you or the guttersnipe. Now, enough with the pampering. If you can talk, you can walk on your own."

Neve stood her ground. Ian's body was the only anchor she had with her world crashing down around her. The dear old man who ordered Christmas baskets from Fortnum & Mason, who loved 80s rock and occasionally flirted with her, now smirked at her with such malignance it chilled her to the bone.

"But you said I had a day!"

"That was before you brought the bobby into it. Now, I have two hostages, and I won't hesitate to use them; trust me," Terence answered.

Neve shivered. Fear skittered up her spine like hundreds of tiny insects. She clutched to Ian for support.

He was there, he was always there. He had tried to break her in her office; he assaulted her; he knew about Stefan, he had learned somehow about Mark... She snapped.

"I can't! I don't know where to start, I need more time!"

Ian spoke up.

"The Isabella Gardner's pieces have been lost for over twenty years. You can't expect her to find them on a wink. I'm sure we can..."

"Silence."

Red lights flashed through the curtains. Terence moved to the window and peeked outside.

Neve straightened up, eyeing Ian. The detective took his attention from the gun and the old man holding it just long enough to stare at her, and gave her an encouraging nod. She tried to convey with a squeeze of fingers that she didn't understand. What did he expect from her? He just pressed her hand back.

At a loss, she watched the room around her. She'd been there on a few occasions, for tea or to hand over the rent of her office next floor. The half-wall on her right separated the living room from the kitchen. She guessed the door next to the closet hid a small washroom, so it makes the one behind them...

Ian's hand brushed her neck, forcing her to look at the coffee table in front of them instead.

"Don't."

"But..."

"Shush..."

His fingers massaged the base of her scalp, the caress out of place given their current predicament. She wished she could draw strength from it. Sensing the panic growing, Ian opened his mouth once more.

"We don't have a choice, Neve, you have to call Caleb."

She looked at him, baffled. He insisted, "He was working on the location coordinates when we spoke to him in the car. He's probably figured it out by now."

"But–"

It really was a 'but.' She didn't know what he was getting at, and even less how to react. As far as she knew, *Lauren* was working on the imprint, and those seven or so scribbles could be anything. Surely he couldn't…

"Enough!"

Neve saw stars. She landed hard on the couch. Ian pounced, stopping inches from his prey by the sting of steel on his stomach.

"You're a better actor than she is, Detective. But you can't teach an old dog new tricks. You won't call anyone, and if I were you, I'll start working on this little mystery; now."

*

"Hey, Peters, there's a shotgun over there, looks like a Remington 870 whose nose was sawed-off short. Cruel. And a 45 mm Glock 21 over there. Shit, that's Braich's shield…"

"Where the hell is he, then?"

Yuan looked at the ambulance driving away and shrugged, moving to the small crowd that had gathered despite the cold, to ask.

*

He still needed to buy some time, but he was running out of options. Plan A –play possum– and plan B –play along– had crashed and burned. Ian weighed the odds.

Whale pocked his gun harder into his torso.

"Don't be stupid."

"Or what? You'll kill me?"

Neve mewled. For a millisecond, Ian regretted the quip. Then the old man roared in laughter. The barrel drifted away, as he turned toward Neve.

"I like him."

The distraction lasted only a breath. Ian smacked the flat of his hand on his opponent's wrist. The pistol dropped. Whale yelped in surprise but the younger man was already on him. Grabbing one arm with his good hand, he twisted and jabbed his other elbow upward.

His parka cushioned the jab, but not the reaction. Pain burst out in his chest. Ian froze for only a second, but the momentary loosening of the grip was enough. Whale dodged for his gun. Neve pushed the table in his legs to trip him. Both men stumbled to their knees. Ian shouted, "Get out!"

She bolted, but in the wrong direction. Ian groaned. The old man crawled away to untangle himself from him. He couldn't both watch Neve and fight. Pushing onto his feet, he tried to grab Whale. The old man twisted away. Suddenly, a heavy bibelot crashed through the glass.

Ian shielded his eyes but only semi-darkness invaded the room. Shadows would have been an ally, but their adversary knew the battlefield better than he did. Neve seemed to realize the danger too. She dashed for the front door.

He strained eyes and ears to follow their adversary's moves to cover for her. There were too many ghosts surrounding them. He wriggled until he found a chair he thought was close to the back of the living room. Groping confirmed the walls angled behind him. From there, he could narrow his attacks.

His cracked ribs howled when he brought his arm forward. The wildfire that spread with each breath he took couldn't be good news. He wouldn't last long, but how to…

"Help!"

Neve screamed in terror. At the same instant, lights flooded. Half-blinded, Ian noticed only the silver reflection on the blade at her throat, then the shadow behind her.

"Mouse, no!"

Neve lunged in the opening Whale's surprise offered. She sank to her knees, escaping the kitchen knife. Whale pivoted, and the heavy glass bottle hit him straight on the face. The teenager danced out of reach as he collapsed to the floor.

"That's for coldcocking me, Spudfucker."

Neve whined in relief. She pulled the girl on her lap and hugged her hard enough to leave bruises.

Ian tottered forward. He spotted the gun on the floor and bent over to grab it. His vision channeled to a flurry of black and white butterflies, the only spot of color the rivulet of blood on Neve's throat. He clenched his teeth, jaw jutted out.

"We have to get out of here."

Neve peeled off her coat and wrapped it around the teenage girl's frail shoulders.

"My office, we left the door opened, we–"

On the floor, Whale stirred. Ian herded them toward the door.

"The cavalry outside will take care of it. Go."

*

207

Neve sat on the stepladder of the ambulance, wrapped in a silver rescue blanket, watching the police officer change the lock on her front door. Adrenaline had left her raw, and empty, so she did little more than blink when a prostrated Whale was shoved inside a car, handcuffed. Her whole body was too numb to move.

The thermos cup Ian pushed into her hands seemed made of lead instead of plastic. She turned her head to thank him then stopped, stricken by the brutal pulse of pain near her cheekbone. Stormy eyes caressed her head while he lowered himself heavily by her side.

The beverage in her cup was creamy, and sweet-flavored.

"Chocolate?"

"Madeline wanted some. I think she has pushed a chair under the knob of the bedroom or something."

She understood the feeling. All she wanted was to curl under her duvet and forget the world.

"You knew she was going there."

"I saw the door cracked open, then close when he pushed her inside. I just hoped she didn't do anything stupid."

Like clubbing her kidnapper from behind while he held a knife at my throat. Neve dismissed the thought with a shudder.

"Next Valentine's Day, I want you to take me someplace hot, and peaceful, where my only concern will be sunburns and whether or not I need to dress up for dinner."

"Perhaps we should go on a proper date before planning our honeymoon," Ian deadpanned, with enough of a smirk to make her flush.

Even blushing hurt.

He hauled himself up. "A patrol car is going to stay here. I have to report to the station…"

A remark about hospitals and cracked ribs racked her brain. There was a question hiding behind the statement. She found just enough energy to ignore both. She was too exhausted for yet another argument.

"I promise I won't go after the treasure without you."

His stare narrowed, and she realized it was more than a tease. She wanted to find the Isabella Gardner lost pieces, and finally put her brother's memory to rest. She didn't want the terror of the night to be for nothing. Ian groaned.

"I had a feeling you would say something like that."

Chapter 25

Despite her statement, Neve spent the next day cuddled on the couch, checking her emails and updating her website while Madeline watched cartoons. Choosing a new template, deleting spam and flagging the messages she would answer later demanded little energy. That was all she had to spare after a restless night filled with nightmares and hot flashes even two scorching showers had failed to squash.

She scrupulously avoided news trends, and hesitated between a catnap and making more popcorn when a ringtone interrupted Jerry's new plot against Tom. The caller ID was masked. Cold fear grabbed her heart in a vice.

"He-hello?"

'God, you sound awful. Understandable considering the ordeal of last night.'

Her lungs emptied in relief. Madeline shot her a curious glance over her mountain of cushions. Neve waved to shush her and escaped toward the kitchen on shaky legs.

"I'm okay, Lauren."

'Good, so you can come over. I have results I want to show you.'

Neve glanced through the window. She would need a change of clothes, then to drive. The day appeared bright and clear, the sky an electric blue. She could do with some brisk, fresh air. Or not.

"Can we do this another time? I'm not really–"

The line grumbled on Lauren's side. Voices whispered and argued, too low to catch more than disconnected words.

'...Can wait... Brother...'

She didn't want to hear it. She needed more time before she faced Mark's past and mistakes once more.

'...Lead...'

Neve rubbed the tension between her brows, then yielded.

"What about dinner? I'll expect you around six?"

Mouse's head perked up from behind the sofa.

"If Ian's coming, you'd better put something sexier on."

Neve gawped, her face growing alarmingly hot.

"I... Never mind. Yes, Lauren... Yes... Sure, red wine's fine... See you later."

She hung up and glared at the sneering teenager who sneered and plopped their last piece of popcorn into her mouth.

"At least he's decent. If you have to bang someone–"

"First of all, we are not *banging*, and second... Well, whatever we do is none of your business. Now shoo. Make yourself useful, we have company coming."

Yet, while Madeline groused about chores, slavery, and the Fifth Amendment, Neve did change into a clean pair of jeans and a striped cotton blouse. Just because looking good boosted her confidence, and Lauren's undertone suggested she would need it.

Ian's eyes narrowed on the pointed collar that concealed the skin-colored Band-Aid on her throat before he landed a light kiss on her cheek and greeted Madeline.

"Hi, kiddo."

"Don't *kiddo* me. I saved your ass. Twice."

"Language," Neve scowled while she checked inside the oven. Ian peered at the bubbling lasagna then glanced back at the girl.

"You saved our *lives*. So here."

Neve frowned at the envelope he put on the table.

"What's that? Money?"

"Start over."

Madeline picked up the letter and read. Her eyes widened, two brilliant onyxes jolting from the page to his face and back.

"No more foster care? Ever?"

"Not if you don't want to."

"Will I have to go to school?"

The flash of hope behind the grouch was unmistakable.

"Well, you'll need some tutoring first, to make sure you're up to eighth grade, but yes. Mom will see to it."

"Your mom? Will I have to go and live with her? Where is that anyway?"

"She lives in a cottage near the Manor. But that's up to you where you want to stay. This document makes you a nation pupil. The government will cover your education and housing, until your majority, as long as you stay in line," he warned.

Madeline opened and closed her mouth in awe. Neve touched his hand, while the girl digested the information.

"How did you–"

"Apparently, Whale was pretty popular with both Bourque and the FBI," Ian said. "His real name was Terence Mailey. Interpol suspected him of smuggling military gear and weapons in Ulster. They've tried to nail him after a pretty nasty case in Ireland about twenty years ago, but he 'disappeared.' So I traded a very detailed statement from the three of us for some witness arrangements for Mouse. New ID, and the like... Wow!"

Neve grabbed his face and planted a sound kiss on his lips.

"You're not the self-centered, arrogant, sexist jerk I first credited you for. Thank you!"

"Is there a compliment somewhere in that list?"

His good arm sneaked around her waist, fingers playing with the fabric.

"Oh please..."

Ian arched an eyebrow at the importune complainer.

"I'll do it, but only if you two stop pawing at each other. We're going to eat here..."

"I second that. Good evening."

Neve stepped out of Ian's grasp to greet Lauren and Luke, who juggled with a wine bag and his crutches. Just as he was to join them, Madeline gave the detective the quickest hug, then slid out of reach faster than an eel to steal a piece of bread and dip it in a mixture of olive oil and vinegar.

"You're welcome."

*

"I still don't see how this *badge* will lead us to the missing art pieces."

Ian leaned back in the couch. Near the window, Madeline sneered, though her gaze never left the traffic in the street below. Neve wondered what she really thought; about Mark; about her naivety; about the possibility of getting off the street... A masculine hand called her attention back to the subject. She was glad her ponytail covered the goose bumps his fingers trailed along her collar.

Lauren typed a command impatiently on her keyboard. The HDMI connection translated it on the TV screen.

"When we realized the bar code from the notebook was an ID, we focused on the logo above. The imprint is too vague for the database to make anything of it, but that particular shade of blue and form match only three logos in vogue in North America: Aero Mexico Airlines, the Cowboys, and the US Postal Service."

"Mark worked as a postman for a while... I remember the bicycle."

Neve bit her lip as she smothered the memory of rides and ice cream on a summer long-gone. Lauren plowed on, "That's what his file says. From December 1989 to July 1991..." she trailed off.

Luke glimpsed at his partner then added, "He was suspected of petty thefts. Some parcels never reached their destination. Mandates were cashed out twice."

Ian interrupted the lengthening list.

"So where does this leave us?"

"To the numbers," Neve whispered.

Lauren beamed, and teased, "Ah, you saw the light..."

"A little explanation would be great for those of us who remain in the dark. What's so special about the numbers?"

Her interest piqued, Madeline crept closer to the party, apparently focused on the difficult task of selecting a biscotti from the plate on the coffee table. Neve swiveled toward Ian, recognition warming her cheeks.

"It's a tracking number. Nicholas explained that Mark was in charge of hiding the treasure, and that their boss had been caught. He had to dispose of the treasure but the exit they had planned was blocked. So he mailed it."

Ian jerked.

"Excuse me? He *mailed* it?"

"Shit, that's *brilliant*!"

Three pairs of eyes glowered at Madeline who bit into her biscuit, indifferent. Neve looked back at the figures on the screen. They'd been so caught up in the mystery they hadn't even noticed the sequence wasn't mirrored. It should have been, as an imprint...

"So brilliant that we don't know jack about the receiver," Ian minced. Luke shrugged.

"We tried the obvious and the tracking system. Now, the system requires ten figures, and we have only seven. A phone call was equally useless."

"Mail is under federal jurisdiction," Madeline piped, as if she was already studying for her next civic's class exam. Ian smirked.

"Good thing we know a federal agent, then."

"Oh no. Absolutely not. I've got enough of Martin snooping around my business. I'll do it."

Ian's hand froze on her neck.

"You're incorrigible. Even after all that happened–"

Neve pulled away from his touch.

"It's my job. I've done it before. There's no need to use force or threaten some poor administrator. Clerks are always happy to help when you ask politely, and smile. And if we're wrong..."

She trailed off, unwilling to word the consequences just yet. Agent Martin might, with luck, forget about the first insult, but he would not be that forgiving if they pulled him into a wild goose chase.

Luke shot a warning glance at Ian and asked, "What do you suggest, Neve?"

"Just what I said. I'll go to a local services provider instead of an official post office, and I'll ask."

"Your track number dates from the nineties. How are you going to explain that?" Ian countered.

"I'll tell the truth. That I found it in my brother's papers, and that he and my parents died when I was a little girl."

*   -

Ian agreed to her plan, on only one condition. Someone was to go with her, as back-up. He then assigned Luke to the task, pretending Nicholas was not to be trusted, and he would not have the patience to cope up with the cajoling. Neve suspected he didn't want to see her trifle with some random clerk. She was female enough to be pleased by the thought, and amused by the fact that the clerk's tag read Lindsay, and that Lindsay – generally, people call me Lindy– was young and pretty and ogled at Luke shamelessly while chatting about siblings.

"Oh, that's so sad… I have two brothers, I'm in the middle, you know. They're a pain in my… But I don't know what I would do without them."

Neve nodded in understanding. The girl took another glimpse at her escort. Well, in Love and War… She slightly pushed the cop forward with an angelic smile.

"Yes, we really miss him, Luke and I. It's just the two of us now."

Lindy perked up as she drew the wrong conclusion, and beamed at Luke.

"Well then, do you have your receipt?"

"No, only the number."

Neve handed the clerk an enhanced copy of the notebook page. The girl's face fell.

"That's really an old number… I'm not sure the system is going to recognize it."

She paused just long enough to confirm the barren search.

"Okay, let me try something else."

Her fingers danced over the keyboard, adding zeroes and asterisks to the original seven digits. Luke craned his neck to watch the half-turned screen when the clerk frowned.

"What does it say?"

The girl continued typing with a frown.

"The last name is Lass, isn't it?"

"Yes."

Neve stepped forward in turn, unsure if Lindy's pout was a good thing or not.

"Is there a problem?"

"Ah! No, not at all..." She flashed another dazzling smile at Luke. "The system took a while to recognize it, because I was trying to track a package sent by your brother. This is a pick-up receipt."

"Pick-up?"

"Yes. But he never came to collect it. Maybe he just forgot, or took too long. We are very strict about–"

The clerk's mouth snapped closed, and her eyes glazed over.

"Oh God, he died... I'm so sorry, I wasn't thinking."

Neve offered a curt nod.

"What happens when a parcel is not collected?"

Happy for the diversion, the girl activated a printer under the counter.

"Well generally they are shipped back to the sender, and if the sender can't be reached, we store them away. I can give you the address of the storage depots, but you'll need to clear it up with the central office first. Here."

Lindy scribbled the address on a Post-it then stuck it to the list she had just printed. Neve scanned the list and chuckled bitterly.

Luke glanced over her shoulder at the one line she was pointing at.

"You've got to be kidding me..."

Chapter 26

Ian straightened up on the sofa. The new bandage around his ribcage was too tight, and itched. Anyhow, the discomfort was a small price to pay to watch Neve fiddle around her office. He smiled up his sleeve when the beautiful PI cracked the door open so she could peek at the corridor for the fifth time.

"Curiosity killed the cat, you know."

Neve ignored the jape, and walked to the window to glimpse outside, marched to her desk, adjusted the chair one inch to the left, and then paced back to the door. Ian caught the hem of her open shawl cardigan before she started a new circuit.

"Why don't you sit down for a breath, and explain again why you feel compelled to wear out your carpet pacing?"

He marked his question with a light tug on the fabric, which brought her between his legs.

"And the best place to sit is your lap, of course?" Neve huffed. Ian smirked.

"Harassing a police officer... That might cost you."

"You're on leave."

The retort wheezed by his cheek as she straightened up and resumed her patrol.

"Neve…"

"Fine! Fine. Martin requested a copy of everything, the notebook, Lauren's files, and then he told me to meet him here at 2:30 pm, since the archives are just next door."

Ian checked his wrist watch.

"We're early. It's barely 2:15 pm."

Unfazed, Neve closed her routine and began another. He stopped her again, more firmly this time and pulled her down beside him. She sighed, "I can't believe it's next door! All this time, it was just here, right under our noses…"

"We don't know yet if the Isabella Gardner lost artwork is there."

She leveled brilliant, tawny eyes with his. The golden sparks in them mesmerized him.

"They are. I know they are. Why else didn't Mark go and collect the package? He knew it would be stored away until he asked for it." She flipped hair out of her eyes. "What time is it?"

Neve grabbed his wrist before he could gather his thoughts, and twisted his arm to look at his watch.

"Hey, that hurt…"

Guileless amusement flickered over her face.

"Poor baby, want me to kiss it better?"

The tease came out of a definitely catlike sneer. Ian grinned back. He thought about kissing her ever since he entered her office an hour ago, and found her already fidgeting like a cat around water. The combination of nerves and grace was mysterious and appealing. Strange, considering that less than a month ago, he dreamed about ditching her in a bottomless well on a regular basis. Her lips curled up a little more, tempting him. He'd be damned if he let her have the last word.

"Well, since you're offering…"

A noise stopped him as he pulled her closer. Neve sprang to her feet. Ian grouched about bad timing under his breath, and stood without enthusiasm.

The trio beside the door barely spared them a glance. Martin waited while a woman whose salt and pepper braid somersaulted each time she flipped a page of the papers she was scanning. That one, Ian guessed, was definitely not happy for the Sunday's disturbance. A small man with a short boxed beard and a neck scarf smiled at Neve.

"Will Hijk, with the Isabella Gardner Museum."

"Doctor Hijk is here to ensure that the paintings, if we find them in this depot, are properly taken care of until we can authenticate them," Martin specified, before he coughed discreetly. The US postal inspector ignored him, probably to make a point, delaying a few extra second before she finally glanced up.

"Everything seemed to be in order. However," she glared at the four people gathered in the corridor, "your mandate covers only the one item described here. I won't tolerate any other tampering."

"That goes without saying, Chief Officer Hog."

The sarcasm clashed with a steely look.

Hijk rubbed his hands, talking to no one in particular.

"I must say I'm particularly excited. Did you know that the *Storm on the Sea of Galilee* is Rembrandt's only known seascape? And the Vermeer… There are so few of them… Ah, if those treasures are here, what a–"

"Let's not get ahead of ourselves, Doctor. We need to find that package first. Chief Officer Hog, if you please?"

One look at the dozens of shelves, overstuffed with envelopes, boxes and dust, sufficed to make Ian grunt.

"Please tell me that all this mess is filed somehow."

The US postal representative minced, "This is a depot, what were you expecting, pins and labels?"

"It wouldn't hurt."

"Ian…"

Neve stepped from behind his back and further into the room. She offered a peaceable smile around.

"Chief Officer, where do you think we should start?"

The woman shrugged.

"I've never been in charge of that particular storehouse. It closed before my time."

With that, she turned her back and focused on a pliable chair she snapped open by the door.

Ian sighed. Searching this room was going to take forever, and nothing guarantied Mark's parcel was stored here. Martin put his phone back in his inside pocket.

"Give me a little credit, Detective. This is the only depot the US postal used in the nineties. Shall we?"

Without waiting for an answer, he proceeded along the rows to the back of the room. Hijk trotted after him, which left Ian to pair with Neve. She wandered in the opposite direction, unsure where to begin.

The hope that had been vibrating inside her for hours wavered. Neve selected a yellowish envelop on a shelf, then another, half-hearted. Ian guided her away gently toward another shelving unit.

"We are looking for a tube."

"A tube? Why?"

"A flat portfolio would have been too big and unpractical. I think your brother rolled the canvases together and disguised them as a set of drawings of some sort."

She bobbed her head, unconvinced.

"Come on, let's try this way."

Ian couldn't blame her for feeling down. Even with a battalion, it would take days to track their prize, whereas they were only four. He suspected Martin preferred to keep a low profile, in case their chase came out fruitless. In the agent's place, he would have done the same: hold back, alert only a few people, so that a failure wouldn't sting that much. And if you were successful…

"Ian, a little help here…"

He snapped out of his reverie to find her clinging to a steel pole, one foot on the lower plank, and the other balancing in the void.

"What on earth are you doing? Get down, you're going to hurt yourself."

His ribs protested when he secured her position with one arm then lifted her away and up. Her hipbone bumped into his shoulder. Ian hissed between clenched teeth.

"Sorry! Sorry…"

She let herself glide between his arms until her toes reached the floor. Ian pressed his forehead against hers with a tentative intake of air that partly eased the pressure inside his chest. Neve fastened her hands behind his neck and repeated, "Sorry… You're okay?"

Her body leaning on him reduced the searing pain to a tingle. He took a deeper breath.

"I could use that kiss now…"

Her amber eyes melted into a sparkling pool. Her fingers played with the short hair on his nape and flared pleasurable quivers on his skin. She was too good at this. Ian relaxed his grip on her waist.

"Ah well, perhaps later. Let's see if we can find a ladder; they must have one somewhere…"

Her disappointed moue almost won him over. Ian murmured against her ear, "Next time I kiss you, I want to be able to enjoy it fully, and without an audience."

Neve's frown lightened and she consented to step away.

As if on cue, they heard Hijk instruct Martin to be careful.

"Get it down slowly, please… Is it the right number? Are you sure? Let me see."

The two men put an extendable plastic tube about seven inches in diameter on the floor. Hijk fumbled with his coat and brandished a flexible tailor ruler. The little man muttered as he measured the length of the tube.

"Fifty-three inches… That's very close, the *Storm*'s smaller side is 49 5/8 inches."

Neve knelt beside him to look at the half-erased label. The seven digits matched Lauren's reconstruction of the tracking number. She nodded to Ian, a little pale. The detective turned to the federal agent.

"Are you going to open it?"

"Yes. The mandate allowed me to take the art pieces out of here, but nothing else."

Hijk bolted to his feet.

"Opening the tube here, in less than pristine conditions? This is madness! In a portfolio, at least we could have had a glimpse, but I can't accept that we risk whatever is in that tube. Out of the question, I forbid it."

"We talked about the risks, Doctor Hijk. I don't have a choice."

"You think this contains some lost artwork?"

The forgotten US postal representative eyed the tube with a mix of awe and suspicion. Martin acquiesced. She asked the art expert, "And you say that opening this here might damage its content?"

"Yes, Mevrouw."

The courteous little bow won Hijk a shy smile. Ian and Neve exchanged a look.

"Let me see that mandate again, Special Agent Martin."

Martin obeyed without a word. She barely took a glance at the document before she handed it back.

"This orders the US postal service to offer you its assistance in securing package number 7651248. Doctor Hijk affirms that opening it in such conditions might damage whatever it contains. It's my prerogative to ask you to take it to a laboratory for further examination."

Neve exhaled. Hijk's reaction was more exuberant. He grabbed the woman's hand in both of his, and shook it until she winced.

"I can't express how–"

The rest got lost as Martin gathered the forgotten tube on the floor and marched toward the door. Hijk released the poor woman's hand and hurried after the federal agent, tearing his ear off with warnings and concerns.

Ian smiled at the two women.

"Thank you for your time, Chief Officer Hog."

The woman gave her braid a little pat, then spun on her heels to exit the storeroom.

*

Hijk agreed to proceed at the police's forensic facility, so two hours later, they all retained their breath behind surgery masks, while the art expert donned a white blouse and a pair of cotton gloves.

"Miss Lauren, if you would be so kind as to dim the lights?"

Lauren almost bounced toward the switch. She flicked it off, and the room took a warm glow. Hijk had explained at length how UV radiation and humidity damaged works of art, altering colors, accelerating cracking, or favoring the growth of the most merciless enemy of all: bacteria and fungi.

"We can only hope the screw lid provided a tight air lock. It would limit the risk of oxidation and the fading of sensitive pigment even though plastic is sadly porous.

I'm wary about the change in temperature. Severe variations induce stress and cracking. Oil paintings on canvas are particularly sensitive, the varnish they used at the time—"

"Doctor."

Martin's stern voice brought the scientist back on track.

With an exaggerated gasp, Hijk started to unscrew the lid. The plastic screeched, rising goose bumps up Neve's arms. She barely allowed herself to breathe, as if the faintest wheeze could sap the ongoing operation.

One last turn, a little pull, and the lid bumped on the counter. Lauren passed over a pair of forceps with rubber ends. Hijk shook his head.

"I'd like a look inside first. Do you have an inspection camera?"

"This is a forensic lab, doctor, name your poison. If you give me a minute, I'll connect the endoscope to this monitor here, so we'll all have a better look."

Ian leaned toward Neve and murmured, "They get on like a house on fire."

"Shush... Oh, my God, look!"

The monitor relayed a dark gray image. Lauren typed a command on her computer, and the image cleared.

"God zij dank... God be blessed... " Hijk almost simmered in pleasure. "The paintings were rolled with the face out and... Yes, it looks like filmy plastic! Whoever did this knew at least the basics about protecting artwork."

Neve shuddered. Martin interfered to dampen the scientist's enthusiasm.

"Can you confirm if that's what we are looking for?"

Hijk sighed noisily, but everybody in the room could tell he was as anxious as the FBI agent to know if they had found the Rembrandts. He pulled the inspection camera out of the tube and adjusted his gloves.

"Miss Lauren, the forceps if you please."

Silence swallowed the room once more. Hearts raced faster with each ruffle. Hijk almost jumped out of his skin when Ian pulled a stool to sit, and scratched the floor doing so.

"Right... I feel like a doctor about to deliver a reluctant baby... Almost there... Ah!"

Dried by more than twenty years of confinement, the plastic plummeted and bared a man drenched in vivid white foam clinging to the ship mainsail, praying that Christ would appease the Storm on the Sea of Galilee.

Epilogue

Neve nibbled at one end of the *bouchée* she'd picked up on the buffet. The jalapeno spice scorched her palate, worsened by some mouthwash aftertaste. She grimaced, looking around for a discreet way to get rid of the sandwich. No such luck. The gallery had stored away garbage cans and decorative plants for the occasion. She sighed, self-conscious of the ridiculous image her grape V-neck one shoulder chiffon dress gave, with a stupid, disgusting bite as an accessory.

She was left with only two options: swallow the rest of it without breathing, or cross the room with her half-eaten sandwich in hand to throw it away in the ladies' room. Neither solution particularly appealed to her.

A small plate appeared in front of her out of nowhere.

"Peppermint relish doesn't go with your gown."

Neve spun on her heels to face her savior. Ian gave the plate a little shake, his customary smirk in place.

"Thank you."

"Don't mention it; I had to rescue Doctor Hijk from a crab and pomegranate stuffed canapé a minute ago. It wasn't pretty."

She glanced above her shoulder, suddenly remembering she hadn't seen any of her party in a while. Ian magically managed to dispose of the offending food under a bench. Neve stifled a laugh.

"I should have thought about that…"

He snatched two flutes of champagne on a passing tray, and offered her one.

"I have no idea what you're talking about."

"Of course not."

She let him escort her through the Raphael Room and the short Gallery, *en route* to the center of the attention for the night, the Dutch room. The wood panels gleamed in the late afternoon light, the windows opened to the balmy April air. It was sinful, to stroll around all that beauty in a pretty dress on the arm of a handsome man, especially when said handsome man had gazed at her open-mouthed when she stepped out of the restroom earlier.

Ian knew how to amuse, charm, or frustrate her, and used his power at will. Tonight, she was charmed, and enjoyed every minute.

They stepped in a small alcove in the Tapestry Room that overlooked the Courtyard. A pianist ended Liszt' Sonata in B minor with a flourish and launched into Schubert's *Wanderer Fantasy*. Ian abandoned his glass on a nearby table, so he could use his now free hand to enlace her.

"Ah, here you are…"

Ian grumbled in her hair.

"I'd really like to be able to kiss you without being interrupted nearly every damned time…"

Neve squeezed his shoulder and beamed at the interloper.

"Doctor Hijk, how are you?"

"Wonderful, wonderful… As I mentioned to Detective Braich earlier, I'm so glad you could join us tonight."

"So are we, Doctor."

Neve ignored Ian when he whispered "I'm not" in her ear. Willem Hijk continued to ramble, "It's all very exciting isn't it? The restoration went on a fast track, but I'm very proud of the job we pulled. You'll see, Degas' gouaches are nearly as good as new, and the Rembrandts, ah, heer Rijn probably would be proud. The *Chiaroscuro* my friends, amazing, simply amazing… Come, come, see for yourself, they're about to lift the curtain."

The energetic art expert tugged them out of their refuge into the spotlight. Hijk excused himself and skittered toward the front of the crowd. Neve sipped her champagne, unsure if the flutters in her stomach were due to the bubbles, or Ian's hand playing with bare skin on her back.

The curator took the stage. Flashes crackled and cheers of applause buried the pianist's efforts. In the background, Martin looked utterly uncomfortable in his tuxedo. Neve sighed.

"I wish we had found all of them, the bronze pieces and the Flinck's oak panel as well."

"No other trace of anything sent by your brother was found. Who knows? The FBI believes some of the stuff was shipped to Philadelphia. Maybe that's it. But before you go on another reckless adventure on a whiff, remember I still owe you dinner."

The frenzy of the last two months had kept them from having a formal date, despite several tries including a couple of lunches interrupted by journalists and art enthusiasts, at least three movie nights cut short by a call from the police central, and one particular embarrassing moment when Ian's mother had come up to his apartment to gather Kermit too early.

"What you owe me, Ian, is a vacation on a paradisiac island."

Ian considered his retort while she curled one hand around his elbow.

"Well then, give me ten minutes so I can talk my brother-in-law into loaning me his yacht. He's anchored somewhere near the Greek islands."

Bronze and molten gold flickered to light her eyes at the mention of the Mediterranean gems, Ian noticed.

"And how long do you need to explain to Madeline why we'll miss brunch at your mom's next Sunday?"

"Oh, we'll be back before lunch."

More applause, some gasps, and the crowd moved forward to admire the recovered artwork. Her long dark curls cascaded down her back when she laughed.

"I'm not crossing an ocean for less than two days."

"Does that rule apply to crossing the Long Island Sound?"

"To the Hamptons?"

The hopeful sparkle brightened her eyes once more. Ian watched people agglutinate around Hijk and the restored artwork, gaping and pointing fingers like children at a zoo.

"You see, I might have packed our stuff and checked out of the hotel…"

"You packed my things?"

"Darling, I've seen enough of you to handle a toothbrush and a pair of jeans… Which leads me to a very intriguing number I found–"

"Shut up, Ian."

"Did I mention you look absolutely stunning in that dress?"

"Kind Sir, lead the way…"

While they made their escape, Luke clasped his fingers with a smug grin. Lauren scowled at her brother and Nicholas.

"You cheated, he tipped you off."

"Claws in, sis. A bet's a bet. They stick around for less than an hour, Nick wins, you lose. Show the money."

"Excuse me?"

The trio turned toward a leggy blonde in a blue silk sarong.

"I was told you could tell me where to find Neve Lass?"

Nicholas' smile broadened.

"I fear she just left, but I'm her assistant. Let me buy you a drink, and you'll tell me how we can be of service."

Ian glanced over his shoulder while Neve donned her cape. He snorted and she laced their fingers together.

"So they did have a bet going on. Who won?"

"Remind me to make my partner pay for lunch next week. Though it seems Nicholas has a price of his own."

She began to turn, which he forbade with a light kiss on her knuckles.

"Next week."

"All right. Next week."

The end is the only the beginning.
February 2014

Also by Claude Dancourt

The Right Place Universe
  Second Chances
  Moonshadows

Return to Caer Lon

>+<

Claude Dancourt lives in Montreal, and wherever her job as an engineer takes her. She is fascinated by books and museums and collects quotes. To discover more about MOONSHADOWS, Claude Dancourt's work, or simply to drop her a word, visit her website:

www.claudedancourt.webs.com